THE NUTCRACKER

CHI VARNADO

GnomeWood Press
P.O. Box 404
Ramona, CA 92065
GnomeWoodPress.com

Cover illustration by Nora Read Coats
Book cover and interior design by Monkey C Media
Edited by Adrianne Moch

First Edition
Printed in the United States of America

ISBN: 978-1-7341423-2-7 (Trade Paperback)
ISBN: 978-1-7341423-3-4 (E-Pub)

Library of Congress Control Number: 2020910733

For Kya and all who dream of dancing:

Bring your world into the dance!

Other books in series

THE NUTCRACKER BALLET STORY

Act One

The Romantic ballet, The Nutcracker, takes place in the winter of 1892. Herr Drosselmeyer, a magic clock maker and creator of mechanical dolls, hopes his goddaughter, Clara, will help him break an evil spell. Her family's annual Christmas Eve party provides the perfect opportunity. The story begins as Clara's parents, Dr. and Mrs. Stahlbaum, welcome their guests. Herr Drosselmeyer is the last to arrive. He brings some of his life-sized dolls to entertain the children. He also has a special wooden Nutcracker for Clara. Her little brother, Fritz, is jealous and snags it from her. Drosselmeyer quickly retrieves it for Clara, for this is no ordinary toy.

As the fantasy unfolds, huge mice appear in Clara's living room. The Christmas tree grows to gigantic proportions. Soldiers battle the mice. The Nutcracker comes to life and fights the ugly Mouse King. Clara tries to help the Nutcracker and, finally, the Mouse King falls. The Nutcracker's spell is broken and a handsome prince emerges.

Act Two

The Prince and Clara go on a magical journey and they soon meet the beautiful Sugar Plum Fairy and her Cavalier. In the kingdom of sweets, the Sugar Plum Fairy and her entourage of delicacies from all over the world pay tribute with magnificent entertainment in the young couple's honor. Eventually, the magical time must come to an end, and they bid farewell.

DANCESPIRATION

Dance and let it go!

"Let it go, let it go—" If we keep our feelings bottled up inside and continue to let them fester, chances are we'll end up blowing off steam at some innocent bystander or make ourselves sick with the poison this creates. Exercise, I believe, is one of the best medicines we have and often just what the doctor orders. So, if you're having a bad day, or hey—even if you're having a great day: put on your favorite music and dance it out. That's right; shake your booty a little. Feel those negative thoughts spin away with each *pirouette*, strike them out with a forceful *frappé*, and sail over them with every *grand jeté*.... You get the picture. Dance, dance, dance and let it go!

—Love,
Miss Chi

"There is no singular way to describe Chi Varnado. As my dance teacher for 9 years she was not only an incredible dancer, but also created a safe, supportive, and community based dance studio that allowed dancers to find themselves and become artists. Her book captures this essence of a place that becomes a home for the many dancers that tell their own stories there. *The Dance Centre Presents The Nutcracker* is a fun story with lovable characters that will have you reading nonstop!"

 —Helen Buchanan, Student at UC Berkeley

"Beautifully written book! Just enough thrill but with a warm cuddle up next to the fire feel. Definitely a must read for any dancer or non dancer!"

 —Emme Chisholm

Contents

1

THE BEACH PARTY

Brindle

To live is to dance.

Brindle senses the strong current forming behind her. Quickly, she kicks her legs. The momentum of the wave is building. Her heart beats faster and she grabs the boogie board, white-knuckling it, and scoots her weight farther back when the front edge dips. It's a good one.

And then her legs pull back—then downward. The pressure in her chest increases and suddenly there's no air. She holds her breath as the force of the wave above pushes her body down farther. Pinned on the ocean floor, hard shells and seaweed poke into the soft skin of her belly. She presses as hard as she can, with all her might, trying to do a push-up. It's not working.

Is this the end? Is this how I'm supposed to die? I always thought I'd be old and decrepit and then pass from old age.

Her lungs are practically bursting from lack of oxygen and thoughts spin out of control while the ocean above thunders wildly.

I'm usually so calm—and in control. I've never had a panic attack before. Is this what it's like? Am I having one now?

An overwhelming sense of doom envelopes Brindle. The cold, watery world closes in around her as she considers giving up. But she decides to give it her all—one last time. She brings her knees up under her and presses off the ground as hard as she can. Finally, the peak of the pressure passes over and she surfaces—*at last!*

Brindle struggles to stand up, gasping for air, just in time for another wave to knock her forward into its grip. She flails her arms and desperately tries to resist, to no avail. It takes her down again, submerging her in its clutches.

Oh, my gosh! How can I get out of this? Usually, everything makes sense—but not this!

Luckily, this one's not quite as strong and she's able to surface again before it's too late. She comes up sputtering and coughing and turns around so she'll see the next one coming. There aren't any more, at least for now, other than the small swells moving toward and then past her. She coughs forcefully, clearing her lungs for a decent breath.

Air—air—I need air! Why is my heart still racing? Is this a panic attack, or a heart attack?

She attempts to calm herself with slow, deep breaths, but only more coughing ensues. *It's not working.* A dark premonition shadows her thinking and slowly reveals itself.

Everything is going to change. The belief of having control is an illusion.

An awful foreboding creeps over her as she stands panting in the surf, now aware of Sophia and Deanne at the shore.

They caught the same wave I did, didn't they? How come they didn't get sucked under like me? Why wasn't I so lucky? Usually so on her game, Brindle now rocks dizzily with the current pounding around her. *Something else bad is going to happen, isn't it? Is this question for God or the universe? I feel so alone.* This isn't exactly a new feeling for Brindle, the alone part anyway, but she'd always felt like she'd had control. This is different.

She lunges forward, taking long strides toward the shore, even though her breath is still shaky. Brindle can't get out of the water fast enough.

"Hey, what took you so long?" Sophia asks. "We thought you caught the same wave as us."

"It was a really good one, too," Deanne says, grabbing Brindle's board as it washes up.

Brindle stares at them, searching for words.

"Well?" Deanne asks.

"I did. I mean, I didn't." The jitters are still getting the best of her. "I got pulled under," she finally sputters.

"Huh?" Sophia moves closer.

"I got held down by a wave and couldn't get up."

"Really? That sounds scary," Deanne says.

"That happened to me one time, too," Sophia says. "It *was* scary!"

"Are you okay now?"

"I think so."

Deanne touches her shoulder reassuringly and Brindle closes her eyes and concentrates on breathing normally. Her heart is still galloping unevenly. *Am I being overly dramatic?*

"Let's go back out," Sophia suggests.

Brindle shakes her head. "You guys go ahead. I'll watch."

The two head out into the surf again and Brindle walks onto the hard sand, but her legs feel like Jell-O and buckle underneath her. She plops down near a seagull pecking at a pile of seaweed. Thin, wispy clouds float gracefully overhead as if nothing has changed, except it has for Brindle. That premonition haunts her. *What is control, anyway? And what is it that's going to threaten me next?* She watches her friends play in the waves until they decide they've had enough. Five minutes later, another wave brings them in.

"That was a blast! Did you see how far I went?" Sophia yells when they wash up beside her.

"We went so far!" Deanne pants. "I can't believe how warm the water is today."

Sophia stands up in the shallow surf and lifts her bright yellow boogie board. "Brindle, didn't you read that it's like seventy-two degrees or something?" Water drips from her long, shiny black hair.

"Yeah, I think so." She'd seen it on the bulletin board by the lifeguard station.

The three musketeers, as the girls are often called, hover in the ankle-deep water. Brindle looks up toward the cement-ringed firepit, and sees people gathering for the evening barbecue.

Brindle watches Randi, Paige, and Marie splash by, trying to catch the boys.

"Slow down! Wait for us!" Marie calls to her boyfriend, Jack. He and Todd are way ahead of them, ducking under waves and pushing their surfboards out toward the break line.

Deanne rolls her eyes. "They'll never catch them."

"Probably not, but it looks like they're having fun trying," Sophia says, and then yells, "*¡Buena suerte!*"

"Good luck?" Brindle asks, feeling a little better now, staring out at the shimmering water all around them. *Sophia's lucky to grow up in a household speaking two languages. Talk about buena suerte.*

"*¡Sí!* You're getting good at this."

Brindle rather likes this idea of picking up Spanish on the fly. It's kind of fun.

They walk up to the gathering on the sand. This is the beach party they'd all talked about when they'd last parted, after their county fair performance of *Giselle.* It's also a last hurrah before the end of summer vacation. Several colorful canopies stand back from the wood-heaped firepit, and two tables, piled with food, are set up underneath a bright green shade. The three girls spread their towels on the sand and take turns reapplying sunscreen to each other's backs.

Sophia's bag chimes and she pulls out her phone. "*Mamá—Un momento.*" She turns to Brindle and says, "My mom says my dad can pick me up at eight, okay?"

"So we're not taking you home?"

She shakes her head. "*No sé, pero llamamos despues. ¿Okay?*" She tosses the phone back into her bag. "Mom said he's in San Diego anyway, on his way home from a work meeting or something."

"Okay. I think I'll put on my T-shirt," Brindle says, "before I burn even more." She rummages through her big green and white-striped tote and pulls out an extra-large lavender shirt.

"That's a little big, don't you think?" Deanne frowns and shakes her head. "Someday I'll go shopping with you so you won't look like a homeless person."

"That's not very nice, Deanne. Who made you the queen of fashion anyway?" Sophia pulls at Brindle's short sleeve, which hangs down past her elbow. "It's just a little big, is all."

Brindle stares down at the oversized shirt. "It's fine. I don't really care."

Paige saunters by and smiles, drying her dishwater-blonde hair with a bright yellow towel. "Cool shirt-dress. I like it."

Brindle smiles up at her. "Thanks."

Deanne teases, "Another one with no taste."

Big deal. Brindle knows absolutely nothing about fashion, but she really couldn't care less. *It's not all that important anyway. Being comfortable and fairly presentable is all that really matters. Deanne must be in one of her snarky moods. Good thing she's nice more often than not.* Down at the shoreline, JP, the gymnastics assistant, does five back-handsprings in a row. "That looks so fun, huh?"

"Yeah," Deanne says. "I wish I could do that."

"Me, too. Hey, look at them!" Sophia points at Randi doing a shoulder-sit on Jack.

"Hey, remember when they took that nasty fall last year? It makes me nervous just watching them," Brindle says. "And remember how terrified she was of ever doing that again? But look at her now—it's like she's fearless."

"You know, it's not really that hard," Deanne says with an air of authority.

"Well, it would be for the rest of us. So just keep it to yourself, okay?" Brindle smiles a half-grin at her friend.

"Hey, let's go join them!" Sophia jumps up and pulls Deanne's hand.

The three girls run down to the hard sand and cartwheel into the shallow water. Paige practices the fish dive move with Todd, and Deanne moves closer.

"Not too bad, Paige. Hey Todd, can I have a turn?" Deanne bounces in place, her bright red hair shining in the sunlight.

"Hang on, Deanne," Paige says and looks at her partner. "One more time, okay?"

Todd nods and assumes the position. Brindle thinks he looks stronger than he did last spring, but he still seems kind of gangly, especially with his wet, black dreadlocks drooping into his face.

Paige poses in *arabesque,* making a right angle with her legs, as he places his right hand on her right side and grips her left leg near the knee. She swoops down, a little clumsily, to an arching fish shape and then he brings her back up again.

"It's so much fun!" she squeals.

"Okay, my turn!" Deanne jumps in front of Todd and lifts her left leg behind her. "Ready?"

He positions his hands, swoops her down accordingly, and then dumps her onto the wet sand.

"Ouch! What'd you do that for?"

"I don't know! I'm so sorry. Are you okay?"

"Dude! You gotta go slower. Come over here, Deanne," Jack says.

She goes over and stands in front of him. Brindle and Sophia move back and trail their toes in the shallow water. Brindle giggles accidentally, amused by Deanne's little mishap, since she *is* being a little snarky today.

Jack carries Deanne through the move in slow motion, probably to help her get her nerve back. They do it a couple more times and work up to normal speed.

Todd must have tried it the exact same way with Deanne as he had with Paige, who is quite a bit heavier. Of course, it wouldn't have worked. It's nice of Jack to not have mentioned their size difference.

Randi, in her green, one-piece swimsuit covered with tiny purple kittens, bounds over and jumps onto Todd's back. He gallops around in the shallow water with her giggling. "Giddy up!" she commands him, her ghostly white skin contrasting starkly against his dark, glistening back.

"They look cute together, don't they?" Sophia says. "He's so dark—even for being black."

"He's definitely tanner," Brindle says.

"Mm hmm. Are they together now?"

"I don't know—" Deanne begins, but is cut off.

"Hey, are you dancers hungry yet? Let's get the barbie going!" JP yells and starts them all moving up toward the potluck area.

"What? Are we in Australia now?" Deanne giggles.

They all turn and quickly move toward the food. Annie, the only college-age dance student, is helping some of the moms pour chips into bowls, remove lids from dips, and arrange space for everything to fit.

"Should we light the fire yet, Mr. Boles?" JP asks. "I think we're all about ready for that."

"Yup, I was just about to do that." Randi's dad pulls a lighter out of his back pocket. He proceeds to light the paper and cardboard that lie beneath the kindling and bigger wood nestled in the fire ring.

The flames slowly begin to take hold of the tinder and Brindle finds herself mesmerized by the blues, yellows, and oranges that take on lives of their own. *How beautiful they are, dancing around each other— swirling, climbing, and wrapping in convoluted patterns.* A tiny piece of blackened newspaper floats upward in the smoke and finally disappears into nothingness. She draws an analogy of life and death. *One minute you're here and the next—you can be gone—just like that little, insignificant piece of paper.* Brindle sometimes finds herself lost in thoughts like this, but now she shakes her head to rattle them away.

"Where were you, Brindle?" Deanne teases. "You look a little dazed."

"Just staring at the flames. Don't you ever do that?"

"They are *muy bonitas*," Sophia says, handing bottles of water to Brindle and Deanne.

Willow, Brindle's little sister by three years, races by with her tomboy friend and accidentally spins sand into Brindle's face.

"Hey! Slow down, will you?" Brindle yells.

"Sorry," Willow yells back, already on the far side of the fire ring.

Mr. Boles calls, "Burgers and dogs are ready! Come and get 'em!"

Randi's dad sure is nice.

The boys line up first and heap their plates with the steaming meat. "I'm starving," they bark, almost in unison.

"Haven't you guys heard, ladies first?" Paige asks from her place next in line. "No manners at all." She smiles and shakes her head.

Deanne says, "Well, they probably need it more than we do. They've been out surfing, you know."

Brindle watches Randi smirk at Deanne's remark. But it's true, they were probably getting the most exercise out there, but she knows her friend actually believes men are somehow more important than women—that their needs should come first. *I'm just happy my family understands that all humans are equal.*

Mom walks over to join the line and counters with, "Are you two trying to get away with poor manners? You'll soon have to be more chivalrous when ballet classes start again next week. And step up to be true gentlemen in your roles in *The Nutcracker*." She lifts an eyebrow then grins.

Dancers and parents alike fill their plates and drift to their particular blankets or chairs to sit in a patchwork of small groupings. Randi, Paige, Todd, Jack, and Marie share a large Mexican blanket, while the three musketeers sit on their towels nearby. JP and Annie nibble on carrot sticks at the smaller table, deep in conversation. Brindle's sister and friend huddle together, eating burgers and busily pushing sand around with their feet.

Dad calls over, "Hey Brindle! Did you get some of the grilled zucchini? And a veggie burger?"

"Yeah! They're really good," she yells back.

Brindle had decided to become a vegan after watching the old film, "Forks Over Knives." The movie made some interesting claims such as how other places in the world that eat little, if any, meat have much less cancer, heart disease, and diabetes. She'd been thinking about it for a while, but that did it for her. Hippocrates said to let food be our medicine.

Her family doesn't eat much meat, though, so it hadn't been all that difficult. She looks around at her fellow dancers eating all those dead animals and feels a little grossed out. She considers saying something to her friends about the disgusting food they're putting into their bodies, but thinks better of it.

Sophia tears open a bag of chips and half of them spill onto the sand. "Oops." She laughs and a seagull scurries over to steal a beak-full.

Deanne giggles and tosses a celery stick toward the group of roaming thieves.

They squawk and fly off frightened, but return almost immediately.

The surf pounds in the foreground and the salty breeze brings a slight fishy aroma to the beach. Brindle looks over to Mom's plate and sees a bed of lettuce topped by a salmon fillet. She crinkles her nose, even though that's the one kind of meat she sort of misses. That must be where the smell is coming from, she deduces.

Being Miss Val's daughter brings both pros and cons, but mostly it's a good thing. The Dance Centre is a family affair. They're all involved, even her little brother, Taz, who's only in first grade. And, of course, Mr. Val— as everyone here refers to him. He always helps out with the many tasks associated with their performances, like hanging stage lights and running sound.

Randi walks up to her teacher. "I liked the Dancespiration in your email, Miss Val, and I agree. To live *is* to dance! And—*Nutcracker* auditions are next Tuesday, right?"

"Yes, they are. In fact, it looks like we have a couple new students who will be trying out for parts along with you guys. Won't that be fun?" Mom smiles mischievously.

"Really?" Deanne asks. "Who are they? Do we know them?"

"I'm not sure, but you'll meet them soon enough."

Brindle watches Randi and Deanne squirm. *They must be worried that those new ballerinas might get the leading roles they've been hoping for. Things might get a little interesting, and competitive.* She kind of likes watching Deanne fret. Sometimes she can be a bit full of herself. Brindle relaxes and enjoys the little sideshow since she knows, from experience, that she won't be cast in any starring roles, since she's the instructor's daughter. She finally accepted that fact when she realized what a tricky position Mom is in. *I suppose she can't very well cast her own children in the lead roles if she wants to keep her business going.* Mom is known for being fair and honest. Integrity is of utmost importance to her, and Brindle is learning that sometimes she has to take a backseat, at least as far as ballet roles go.

Deep reds spread across the sky as the sun completes its descent. Brindle glances at the horizon, waiting for it. *Will it happen or not?* It's rare, but she waits expectantly.

"There it is!" she shouts. A flash of green ignites just as the warm yellow orb slips behind the veil of blue-gray ocean.

Dad echoes her enthusiasm. After roasting marshmallows and eating s'mores, the group packs up. School starts the day after tomorrow and auditions are the day after that. Even though she knows she won't be cast as Clara or the Sugar Plum Fairy, Brindle looks forward to ballet starting back and immersing herself in the magical world of make-believe once again.

2

Auditions

Paige

*It's always in your best interest
to put your best foot forward.*

Paige's mother whips into a parking space. "Whew! I didn't think we were going to make it on time!"

They'd come straight from the doctor's office.

A group of dancers and parents mill around the front of the studio. The blues, reds, blacks, yellows, and pinks of her dance family's attire reminds Paige of a field of wildflowers.

We can thank the lack of a dress code for that. But the sight makes her stomach turn with nervous worry. Then again, her stomach has been bothering her, off and on, for the last month or so. *The only upshot to this is that I've dropped a few pounds.*

"Wow. Will you look at all those ballerinas? Everyone's grown up so much since last spring, and it looks like there might be a few new ones, too," Mom says, handing Paige a check already made out to the Dance Centre. "Just bring the paperwork home and tell Miss Val you'll return it on Saturday, okay?"

Paige stares at the mob. "Uh huh. I hope I do okay today, in the auditions I mean." She grimaces, but is glad she got to ride with her mother. "At least the doctor said I don't have the flu, right? My stomach was feeling better, but now I feel a little queasy again."

"You're probably just nervous, honey." Mom puts her hand on Paige's knee. "I've gotta run. I have a three o'clock that I have to get back to the office for."

"Mom, don't you ever get tired of listening to everyone else's problems—on top of mine?"

"Well, I never get tired of you, if that's what you're asking."

Paige leans over and kisses her on the cheek, opens the door to get out, then steels herself for the tryouts.

Miss Val calls the class to order. "Did you all know that *The Nutcracker* was first performed in Russia in 1892? And, of course, Tchaikovsky composed the music. This ballet is over 125 years old!"

"An oldie, but goodie—right, Miss Val?" Todd asks, sitting next to Randi.

"Indeed it is. All right, first we'll do a *barre* to warm up and then a short center routine. After that, a few turns and then you may stretch on your own. I'll be watching all of you and taking notes. All right, let's begin and good luck to each of you."

She proceeds to demonstrate the *plié* exercise at the *barre* and then perches on her stool next to the stereo, watching the dancers in the huge mirrors covering the front wall while taking notes on her clipboard.

Paige is nervous and out of shape as she begins the exercises. *Why do auditions have to be on the first day back after having the whole month of August off?* Her heart is beating way faster than normal, so she closes her eyes during a *port-de-bras* forward and tries to center herself.

"Paige," Miss Val begins. "Don't duck your chin on the way up. It breaks the line from the back through the neck."

She opens her eyes and nods.

As the class continues, Miss Val says, "Relax a little, you guys!" She laughs lightly. "The parts won't be based entirely on today, you know? But you should get used to auditioning. It's a useful skill to be able to perform under pressure. Besides, I know most of you. I know your dancing history. Just do your best, okay?" She looks around at everyone and then down at her clipboard. Glancing up again, she smiles. "And, for heaven's sake, breathe!"

Everyone laughs and the mood lightens. Randi and Deanne are dancing amazingly well. Randi, her best friend in the world, the one who convinced her to join ballet four years ago, has barely even smiled since class began. *She's probably nervous, too. But she's such a good dancer. In fact, she's the best one in class. She rocked the lead role of* Giselle *last year.*

Paige glances at the other dancers as they continue and notices the two new girls. One of them looks like a professional. Her turnout is insane and in a *penché arabesque* her leg goes higher than anyone else's. Deanne is obviously competing with her and Randi, and forces her leg up a notch.

Something's different about Deanne. Is it her leotard or what? Oh, her red hair isn't as frizzy as usual—all tucked up in that donut bun. Yup, she's gone all out here.

Paige can't help but giggle as she drifts back into her usual happy-go-lucky self. She's starting to relax and enjoy the little dramas around her now and catches Miss Val shaking her head with that mischievous glint in her eyes. Paige stops worrying and realizes how good it is to be back. She stands tall and breathes deeply while executing the *grand battements.*

Once the dancers have finished stretching and gotten drinks of water, Miss Val teaches them a short pattern that they will perform, a few at a time. Randi is paired with the awesome new girl; Paige, Deanne, and Sophia are in a group together. Brindle, the other new girl, and Annie form a trio. Jack and Todd follow along in back since they're the only guys. Paige likes the lively music. It's from Vivaldi's *Four Seasons.*

Todd sure is watching Randi a lot. What's going on?

Group one begins the dance as the others stand across the back of the studio. Paige and some of the others mark the pattern in place so they'll know it better when it's their turn. This way, they can use muscle memory as well, in case they forget the steps. Miss Val is always telling them how important this is, since you can't always rely on just remembering alone. When they're learning parts for new dances to perform, she also encourages them to visualize going through the steps while lying in bed before going to sleep at night, and to actively engage their muscles while doing so. It actually does work. Paige did this when she was trying to remember her part as a Wili, last spring for *Giselle*.

The professional-looking new girl, in her bright red leotard and short black skirt, falls out of a double *pirouette* and frowns. But she keeps going, then smiles like she's having a good time. Meanwhile, Randi remains solid in her execution of the turns and connecting steps. She even nails the last pose, a *back attitude en relevé*, and actually holds it for a few seconds! The class members applaud and yell their enthusiasm and as Randi curtsies graciously toward them, Paige notices Todd staring at her friend again.

The other girl tells Randi, "Nice job!"

"You, too."

Miss Val smiles at them and jots notes onto her clipboard. "Group two!" she calls.

Paige positions herself in the front right, with Deanne to the left, and Sophia takes back center. The music begins and the group descends into a *grand plié*, lifting their arms upward into high fifth. After rising, the music shifts to a bright, happy melody and the movements quicken. When the *pirouette* comes, she decides on a single, instead of a double, so she can be sure to stick the landing. In the mirror she watches Deanne attempt a triple, unsuccessfully. The trio travels in a large circle with *sauté, tombé, glissade,* and *grand pas de chat* followed by a single and then a double *piqué turn* to finish the rotation. The double is difficult, but Paige manages to pull it off, barely. In the ending pose, Deanne stays up *en relevé* the longest, but not as long as Randi did. Their comrades also applaud them supportively and the next group gets ready.

Group three does pretty well, Paige observes, and the audition/class continues. Randi seems to be doing great today, while Deanne looks like she's back to trying to compete with her—like last year. *Why can't she just relax and enjoy dancing, the way the rest of us seem to be doing now—even the new girls. But, I guess, it is still sort of a tryout class.*

When the stressful session is finally over, Paige tosses Randi's towel over to her and then mops her own face and neck. "Good job, Randi. You did great today."

"Thanks. You did, too. How are you feeling these days?" Randi's focus pulls briefly away, toward Todd, who's talking to Jack.

"You know, sometimes good, sometimes not so good." Paige shrugs. "The new girls seem nice." She tosses her towel on top of her ballet bag, which is lined up with the others underneath the *barres.*

"Yeah, they do."

"Hey, do you think we could get together this weekend?"

"I hope so. Call me?" Randi walks outside to greet the Beginners who are waiting out front until the

Advanced kids leave. A mother, wearing a professional-looking yellow suit, approaches Miss Val. Her high heels click determinately on the wooden floor.

"Well, what did you think of my daughter? Isn't she fabulous? She's certainly ready to assume the lead in your little production, don't you think?" The woman stands there with a phony smile plastered on her face.

Paige can't help but overhear the conversation.

Miss Val looks up from her clipboard and smiles warmly. "She is a very beautiful dancer. You must be so proud of her."

"Yes, of course we are. So, she *will* be the Sugar Plum Fairy, right?" She holds her gaze on Miss Val.

"There are many things I have to consider when assigning parts. There's no way I can please everyone, so we all have to be good sports about it. Not everyone will get to dance a lead role, but I try to be as fair as possible. And I ask that all the students display good sportsmanship and take on a team spirit. I want to inspire that in these students. It's one of the reasons we don't go to competitions. Does that sound all right?"

By now, the woman's grin has faded and she's backing away. "Well, in that case, I don't think my daughter belongs here. I'll need my check returned."

"But Mom! I like it here. It doesn't matter what part I get! These kids are friendly."

"No, dear. We'll go over and try that other studio. I hear *they* go to *lots* of competitions and win awards. Let's go."

Tears pool in the poor girl's eyes. "Please, Mom?"

"No, honey. We're out of here. Just as soon as I get my check back."

Miss Val rifles through the stack of registration papers, hands her the check and turns to the girl. "I'm sorry it didn't work out here. Good luck wherever you go. You're a beautiful dancer."

The girl nods and obediently follows her mother out the door. The remaining students sheepishly wave goodbye to her as another mom taps Miss Val's shoulder.

"*We're* interested in joining," she says. "My daughter says she loved this class. We came from that other studio. Julie says there's too much drama over there and I think it's way too expensive. Anyway, we're here for good, if you'll have us?"

At least this mom's smile looks real. Miss Val seems relieved. Even though she had remained calm the whole time, talking with that other lady must have been very uncomfortable.

"Thank you," she says. "We'd be glad to have Julie join our ballet family."

Deanne walks up to Miss Val on her way out, dance bag thrown over her shoulder. "When will you tell us what parts we got?"

"Probably sometime next week." Miss Val walks toward the front desk and motions to Randi to bring in the next class. The Beginners won't be having auditions since they'll be part of the bigger group numbers. "You all did great," she calls to the Advanced dancers as they're leaving. "See you Saturday!"

Paige thanks her teacher for the class, like she always does, and squeezes by all the little kids coming in. "See you tomorrow at school, Randi."

Randi waves back at her as Todd leans in for a quick hug before taking off on his bike. She lingers at the door gazing after him. Something tugs on Paige's heartstrings, but she's confused as to what. Finally, her best friend escorts the Beginners away from the doorway, over to sit in a circle in the center. She's been helping Miss Val with the younger ones for years and always talks about how much fun it is.

Paige glances around the parking lot and spots her mom's car. She can feel her legs starting to hurt, but recognizes it's a good kind of sore. It's about time she gets her muscles back into shape. But for now, she's glad to be heading home. She's already got a ton of homework in math and science, and it's only the second day of school.

As she opens the car door, she's greeted by the usual news/talk radio her mom always listens to. They're covering a brush fire that started about an hour ago and is rapidly consuming large swaths of vegetation.

"It's that time of year again, I'm afraid," Mom says. "It sure would be nice to not have this dry weather every fall."

Paige's eyes follow her mom's pointed finger to the mountains in the east. She can just make out a faint plume of smoke dispersing into the late afternoon sky. Again, her stomach clenches, so she pulls her bottle of water out of her ballet bag—if for no other reason than to simply distract herself.

"We should be fine, Paige, as long as Santa Ana winds don't start up soon."

They drive home along the tree-lined street in silence, except for the radio, which continues its ongoing story about the fire.

3

FIRE

Brindle

When turning, close arms below shoulder level and keep each centered—don't let them cross to the other side of your body.

Brindle pulls the large green sweatshirt over her wet blonde hair and pushes each arm through the appropriate sleeve. Her muscles feel nice and relaxed now that she's eaten dinner and taken a hot bath. The audition class this afternoon had been grueling; she's glad it's over with and can't wait to climb into bed. But first, she'd better go outside and say goodnight to their Australian Shepherd, who sleeps on the porch. It's been a nightly ritual and her chance to check in with the night sky and see which constellations she recognizes.

The sky's too cloudy, or something, because not many stars are visible. Plus, there's a lingering smell from that fire out past Palomar Mountain. Nutkins pads over and licks her hand, reminding her to pet him. When she rubs the dog's neck, she feels a shock and pulls back.

"I'm sorry, Nutkins. It's just static electricity. I didn't mean to shock you, boy." She hadn't realized how dry the air was and pets him again, tentatively, before heading back in the house to go to bed.

Brindle's body rocks back and forth as if something is shaking her. "Ugh. No." There's pressure on her shoulder and she squirms to get away. "Nooo."

"Brindle, you need to get up. Right now."

She opens her eyes to the bright lamp light. "What?" It's still dark out.

Mom's voice is shaking. "You have to get up. That fire has gotten bigger and we're evacuating."

That's enough to make me sit up. Willow's already scurrying around the bedroom throwing clothes into a bag.

"But it's so far away. Isn't it?" *My insides twist and suddenly I'm nauseous.*

"We're just trying to play it safe, but you never know. A Santa Ana wind is starting to blow. Just pack some clothes and anything else you think you might need. Okay?" Mom's voice still sounds different.

"All right," she says, hesitantly, as Mom leaves the room. She swings her bare feet onto the wooden floor; stands up, numbly; and stares at Willow. Her sister is like the Energizer Bunny, even now in the pre-dawn hour.

"Hurry, Brindle!" Mom has reappeared in the doorway, but then bustles away.

She pulls on the pair of jeans she wore yesterday and buttons them underneath her nightgown. The kitchen door closes downstairs, and then there's a sputtering noise. She and Willow both freeze and listen through the open window. The roof sprinkler. They open their eyes wide at each other. *Mom or Dad must've turned it on. This is serious!* Willow grabs her bag and rushes out and Brindle begins to pack in haste.

Books! What about all my books? Of course she *has* to take those, or at least the most important ones. She begins pulling volumes off the shelves and before long there are dozens of titles littering the floor.

Dad pops in his head and clears his throat. "Wow, Brindle. You can't take all those. We're in a hurry and won't have room."

"But Dad," she whines. "These are my friends."

"I know, but you'll have to just pick a few favorites and leave the rest." As he heads down the stairs he adds, "Let's just hope for the best."

His voice trails off and Brindle is left on her own to make the painful choices she knows she must. *But how?* She dumps out her old toy box and begins the process. *Pride and Prejudice*: she read that, but it's a keeper. *Wind in the Willows*: that was a long time ago, but she can't let that go. A stack of library books: she stuffs them into a pillow case. *The Red Tent*: she hasn't gotten to it yet, so that goes into the box.

When she runs out of space, she closes her eyes tightly and tries not to look at any more of them. She drags the heavy box and loaded pillowcase out of her room onto the landing and finishes getting dressed.

For the next forty-five minutes, the family fills laundry baskets with photo albums, and packs fresh fruit from the hanging basket, snacks, heaps of clothes—and piles them by the front door. Taz hurries downstairs carrying his guinea pig cage and sets it on the dining room table, next to the laptops and piano books. The two cats, Bonnie and Clyde, meow noisily in a pet carrier and Nutkins whines outside the door.

Mom pulls on a flannel shirt and pauses at the door. "Brindle, keep an eye on Taz. You guys stay inside while Dad and I hook up the horse trailer. Got it?" She doesn't even wait for an answer. She just opens the door and goes out into the darkness.

Dad must already be outside. Brindle fills their water bottles at the sink and tucks them into one of the open sacks on the floor. Willow paces from room to room, picking up things and putting them back down again. *That's not like Willow. She's usually more decisive.* Taz stands at the table, leaning his forehead against the cage, and when he looks up she sees he's crying. *He must be so scared.* She puts her arm around his shoulder, leading him over to the white wicker couch, where they sit down together.

"It's okay, Taz. We're just getting things ready to go. It's very unlikely the fire will come all the way here." *But it could. How horrifying would that be?* "Don't worry. Mom will be back soon."

Dad barges into the kitchen and yanks open a drawer, grabbing a handful of small towels. "Mom wants to hold off loading the horses until daylight, if we can. Taz, you okay buddy?"

Her little blond brother nods, but uncertainly, and squeezes Brindle's hand tighter.

Fifteen minutes later, *but it feels like an hour,* Mom announces it's just beginning to get light. "Jethro, could you take those laundry baskets out to the car while Willow and I halter the horses?"

"Yeah, I'll get 'em." He stacks one on top of the other and follows them out.

Brindle takes the stack of laptops and Taz picks up the cage. Outside, the sky is barely visible, but she can't see any stars. The stench of smoke stings her nostrils. It's *much* stronger than it was last night. Taz follows close behind and they stuff their armloads onto the floor of the Subaru. Willow runs toward the car and throws the last saddle into the back.

A gust of warm, smelly air blows the cowboy hat off Taz's head and it flies up into the tree and gets stuck. "My favorite hat! I need it."

A more powerful wave of wind howls through the canyon and carries dust, smoke, and leaves at a frightening speed. This gust doesn't let up and Brindle guides her brother into the car.

Mom and Dad are each leading a horse toward their rig parked in the middle of the dirt road. The bay mare is the first to go in, followed by the grey gelding. Mom closes the trailer door and wipes her hands on her pants, leaving black streaks. "Let's go!" she shouts, running to hop into the truck with Nutkins and Willow. Brindle and Taz go with Dad, jammed with all the stuff, as they follow the rig out the long dirt road.

Brindle pants. "Where are the goats?"

Dad answers without looking back. "In the front of the trailer."

The two of them bounce along in the backseat as Dad keeps a reasonable distance behind the trailer to not spook the horses. Usually, Mom drives the rig incredibly slow over the ruts, but she's driving faster now in the dawning day. Even allowing for the distance behind, there's an awful lot of dust coming their way.

Or wait... "Is that dust or smoke?" Brindle fights her worried stomach and pats Taz's hand, semi-reassuringly.

"Oohh, maybe smoke?" Dad answers.

Further out the road, beyond the oak canopy of the canyon, the road opens up into a field on the left. Brindle stares out the window at a bright orange ribbon glowing above the mountain beyond the meadow. It flashes intermittently in the not-quite-dark sky.

Dad brakes and also looks over. "Holy moly! That doesn't look good."

"Is it gonna get us?" Taz squeaks out. "I'm scared."

Brindle draws in a shaky breath and Dad answers. "No, son. That's why we're leaving now. We'll be all right. Try not to worry, okay?"

His tone does not comfort Brindle at all. She does *not* want to lose the place she loves more than anything in the world. The trees in the creek bed, the beautiful wildflowers blanketing the meadows, the boulders she pretends are her friends, their beloved home, her piano, books—everything she holds dear in her life.

She glances over again and gasps as a huge wall of flame crests the mountain and heads toward them. A scream escapes her throat and Taz starts to cry.

"Hang on, guys!" Dad presses the accelerator and closes the gap between them and the horse trailer. Mom must have seen it, too, because the rig peels out as she turns onto the main road. Dad jams on the brakes when a car appears out of nowhere. He blows out his cheeks with a trumpet of concern.

The smoke is even thicker here and much more difficult to see through. They follow the slow line of taillights up the windy, rural road that leads into town. Brindle jerks at a loud boom behind them. And then another one!

"What's that?" *Bombs going off?*

It takes a minute for Dad to answer. "I think they're propane tanks exploding." He keeps turning around to look behind them.

"It's so loud," Taz whimpers.

Brindle feels bad for her little brother, being so scared, but it's all she can do right now just to keep from bursting into tears. She doesn't have much to give at this moment, but she takes his trembling fingers into her hand, anyway, and holds them tight. Another boom goes off and she shrinks down low in the seat and closes her eyes tightly.

This must be why people pray, like Deanne is always talking about.

A much louder explosion bangs and the car continues lurching up the road as more and more vehicles pull in from side roads.

It's worth a try. Dear God—if that's even what I'm supposed to call you. Please help us get out of here safely. She opens her eyes and looks over at Taz, who's staring at her. *And please protect our home in the canyon.* Her mind is racing and she's unable to finish a thought. She can't think of anything else to pray for so she signs off, but adds, in her thoughts, *Please, let's keep it open.* Like a phone call—she's afraid to hang up yet.

They pass a couple holding a pony on the side of the road, waving their arms for them to stop.

"It's too bad we're full-up," Dad says. "It's hard not being able to help. There's just no more room, with the horse trailer already full."

Brindle knows he's trying to justify not being able to assist others in distress. "Hopefully, someone will be able to help them," she offers consolingly.

Their long trek into town is painfully slow and nerve-wracking. Brindle senses a migraine coming on and closes her eyes against the real-life scene of flames jumping down the mountain toward them, while the Santa Ana winds rock their car like a boat on a violent sea. And then she remembers that horrible premonition she had at the beach. *Is something bad going to happen? Is it already happening now?*

4

INNER ISSUES

Paige

No Dancespiration this week.

Paige and her mother sit in the crowded room, in the middle of the night, waiting to see a doctor. Her stomach has been bothering her for weeks, but now she's in absolute agony. The ER is not in their hometown of Nuevo, but down in San Diego. They've been staying in a motel in the city since they evacuated two days ago. The fires continue to burn all over the county. Schools and many businesses have closed for the week and ash has settled over everything.

"What do you think is wrong with me? What if it's cancer or something horrible like that?" Paige leans her head against Mom's soft shoulder and blows her nose, for the umpteenth time, into the soaked tissue. *Is this from crying? Do I have a cold? Is it the lingering smoke everywhere?*

Mom strokes her hair soothingly. "It's probably just nerves. Try not to worry so much, sweetie. The smoke in the air alone is enough to make most of us feel sick."

Finally, she's called in and Mom leads her through the open doorway. They follow the nurse into a small curtained-off area where she pulls a new sheet of waxy paper over the table and Paige sits down.

"The doctor will be in soon," she says and quickly exits.

"We know what *that* means," Paige says, rolling her eyes. "It'll be another hour."

Mom sits in the chair, leans back, and closes her eyes. "Try to relax, Paige."

Easy for you to say. You're not the one who's scared to eat anything—afraid it'll come back out, spewing from both ends.

Surprisingly, the doctor comes in fairly soon, wearing a white lab coat and a hearty smile. "So, who have we got here and what seems to be the problem?" He pulls the small rolling stool toward them and eases down onto it.

She grabs her torso and scrunches her face. "I'm Paige and I feel like crap."

Mom takes over from here. "She can't seem to keep anything down and she feels sick most of the time."

The doctor turns back to Paige. "Is it mostly right after you eat?"

She nods and looks at Mom.

"It's been going on for over a month. Our doctor ordered blood work, but that didn't show any allergies and it hasn't improved."

"Does anything make it feel better?" he asks, looking down at his iPad.

"Well, *not* eating, but then I get a headache."

The doctor continues with his questions, palpates her stomach, and then sends them back out to the waiting room until he can schedule a CT scan to rule out appendicitis.

Paige is eating very little since her trip to the ER. At least her appendix is okay. But something is still wreaking havoc with her insides. She never feels all that great and really has to watch what she eats.

Nuevo has now been closed down for three entire days. However, she and her mom have finally been allowed to return home after the mandatory evacuation. They drive down Main Street and the place feels like a ghost town.

"I could actually get used to this," Mom says. "No traffic."

"That's for sure, but I wonder how everyone's doing."

They pull into the 7-11 and see armed guards marching along the street.

"What the heck? Are they expecting Armageddon or what?" Paige watches one guy stare sternly their way. *He's barely older than me.*

"I think it's just the National Guard. Look, he's handing out bottled water to that truck."

They get out of the car to go in the store for whatever food and drinks there are to find, since nowhere else is open.

Mom stops and accepts some free water. "What are you guys doing here? Are you expecting problems?"

"No, not necessarily, ma'am. We're here, you know, just in case." The man nods at Paige. "To serve and protect."

When you're barely out of high school? Paige smiles back, in spite of the summersaults her stomach is performing, and follows Mom into the building. "Let's make it quick, okay? All this gives me the creeps."

"Me, too."

They pick from what's left of the canned juices and pre-packaged, so-called food, and continue their drive home through the smoky haze, sprinkling ash, and nearly empty streets.

Mom pulls the Lexus into the driveway and Paige pulls open the garage door. She notices the difference between inside and outside. It was becoming the norm to have everything covered in a fine dusting of ash. But when she sees the interior of the garage, the bicycles and boxes are not all dusty looking. It looks like when they'd left.

They each start carrying boxes and bags from the car into the house. There is so much stuff they'll have to unpack and put away. Paige almost wishes they hadn't left. That way, they wouldn't have *so* much work to do now, when she feels so crappy. A nap would be great right now, but she knows she should help Mom with the chores.

"Dinner first, okay Paige?"

"Ugh, I don't really feel like it." The thought of eating just makes her worry and then feel nauseous.

Mom sets a bag on the kitchen counter and unloads the cans. "How about chicken and rice soup?"

Paige considers this and rests her hand on her stomach, as if asking her gut permission, or striking a deal with it, or something. "I could give it a try."

"Good," Mom says, pouring the contents into a dish and putting it in the microwave.

Paige decides to eat an apple as an appetizer, usually a safe choice with little chance of consequences.

The two of them sit at their small kitchen table and Paige chews each bite slowly and thoroughly. Out the window she watches the streetlight across the road turn on. The neighbor's car backs out and leaves their block.

"It's good to be home, isn't it?" Mom pulls some crackers out of the wrapper and breaks them up into her bowl of soup. "Would you like some, too?"

Paige shakes her head. "I'm glad to be home, too. I just want everything to get back to normal. No more fires. And me feeling decent."

"I know. You and me both."

Later that evening, she tries to call Randi again, hoping to connect this time. Cell reception has been nonexistent for the last couple days. She's not sure if the airwaves are simply oversaturated with calls or if the cell towers have burned down. This time, she manages to get through and her best friend actually answers.

"Randi, hello! I've been so worried about you. Is everybody okay?"

"Oh, my gosh! It's so good to hear your voice. We're okay. How 'bout you guys?"

Paige learns that Randi's family, who lives across town, didn't evacuate and is somehow relieved. "Have you heard from anyone else? Annie or Miss Val?"

"No, you're the first one who's gotten through."

"I hope everyone's okay."

"Me, too. The only good thing about this situation is that there hasn't been any school this week. But the fires have been *so* stressful, haven't they?" Randi also tells her that Butch, her cat, has been cooped up inside because of all the smoke. "But he keeps trying to escape."

"You and your cat. I know you love him." She pictures her friend's kitty walking along the windowsill, knocking over some of those silly ceramic cats that decorate her room.

"Hey, are you feeling any better?"

"Sort of. Well, sometimes." Paige explains the visit to the ER, where they ruled out appendicitis, but nothing was figured out. She can't help but wonder if she'll feel like this the rest of her life.

"I'm sorry. Maybe your regular doctor will know what's going on."

"No, I've already seen him several times and he keeps prescribing antacids and other stuff that doesn't work. I'm *so* sick of this, literally. But, enough about me. I can't wait to hear about our audition."

"Yeah, me, too."

"It'll sure be good to get back to the way things were before the fire."

"At least the phones are working now."

It's always so nice to talk with Randi. They've been close for a long time. *But she's seemed kind of distant recently. Preoccupied? Even this summer, she didn't call me as much.* Paige wonders what it will be like when they leave for college and don't have each other close by. It's more than a year-and-a-half away, but right now she wishes it was longer.

5

LODGING

Brindle

No Dancespiration this week.

Brindle jolts awake when something scratches her face. "Aagh! What's that?" She throws off the covers and sits up, looking around frantically.

"Wheek! Wheek!" Something brown and white hurls itself off the bed with a thud and scurries into the pile of clothes heaped in the corner of the room.

"What the heck, Brindle! Why are you yelling?" Willow props up next to her.

Why is Willow in my bed? Wait, this isn't even my bed. Then she remembers.

Taz runs through the open bedroom door and closes it quickly. "Did you see Tiger?" he pants. "She got loose and I can't find her!"

Oh, it must have been his guinea pig that ran across my face. And this isn't my room.

Four days later, they are still at their aunt's house, staying until the evacuation order for their area is lifted. She hasn't even been able to talk to Sophia or Deanne due to poor cell reception.

When the pile of clothes rustles, Taz reaches underneath it and pulls out his beloved guinea pig. "Tiger, I'm so glad I found you." He kisses her face; carries the soft fur ball over to his bedroll on the floor; and snuggles down into it, holding his friend tightly.

I wish someone would snuggle me like that. But, I guess I'm a little old for that.

"When do you think we'll be able to go back home?" Willow asks.

Brindle yawns and stretches. "I don't know. I hope soon, like today." She glances over to the dresser and sees a stuffed trash bag taking over the entire surface. "What's in there?"

"What do you think?" Willow says, standing up to pull on jeans underneath her long T-shirt.

Taz puts Tiger in the little cage next to his bedroll and says, "It's full of her Beanie Babies."

"Oh, my gosh, Willow! You actually took the time to collect all those before we evacuated?"

"Of course! I spent a lot of money on them." She ties her shoes and looks back at Brindle. "I wonder what's for breakfast?"

There's a knock and Mom pokes in her head. "How are you guys doing?"

Brindle looks up. "How do you think we're doing? It's kind of crammed in here."

"Can we go home yet, Mom?" Taz asks. "I ran out of food for Tiger."

"That's all right, kiddo. I'm sure Aunt Mary has some celery or something for her."

"Well? Can we go home yet?" Brindle asks.

"Dad's making some calls right now and checking online. But it looks like they're not letting anyone who lives on the west end of town go back just yet. I'm sure we'll know something soon." Mom looks tired and her hair is a mess, tucked haphazardly into an unruly ponytail. "Get dressed, guys. Let's have breakfast. I know there's cereal and fruit, and I'm not sure what else." She drifts out of the room, scratching her head absentmindedly.

Willow and Taz follow her out and Brindle walks over to the window and stares at the corrals in the side yard. Their two horses and three goats are together in one large enclosure, munching on hay; her Aunt Mary's show horses must be in the barn, since she doesn't see them.

This place is okay, nice house, a couple acres, a few neighbors scattered around—yet visible. Home is better, much more to my liking. A hundred acres, mountains and trails to roam, a creek running through in the wintertime, birds galore. *I sure hope that home is still there—waiting patiently for us, untouched by the destruction of fire. A book comes to mind, something I read, perhaps a few years ago? Oh yeah, it was* Little House on the Prairie.

Laura Ingalls' family had worked so hard building their homestead and then along came one of those fast-burning prairie fires that consumes everything in its path. But, in that case, the family worked together and saved their little log house—but barely. Pa plowed around the cabin, and then lit a backfire in hopes of burning the grass between them and the approaching flames. It worked! They threw buckets of water, and slapped wet sacks on the flames. In the end, they were victorious and the fire blew onward—away from their little homestead.

But we didn't stay to fight the fire like they did.

Brindle marches out to the kitchen to join the others. "Why didn't we stay and fight the fire?" Tears sting her eyes as visions of her beloved canyon going up in smoke consume her.

"Honey," Dad says consolingly. "It was too big and coming too fast."

"But Laura Ingalls' family stayed and saved their farm," she sobs. "And they didn't even have running water!"

"That was just a story," Willow counters.

"It's a true story, you imbecile!"

Taz starts to whimper and Dad shakes his head at Willow, apologetically.

"When you live in a box canyon, like we do, you can't stay there. Not with only one way out and canyon walls holding in the smoke. An open prairie is another situation all together. We did what we could."

"Yeah, nothing. Absolutely nothing!"

Mom reminds her they had turned on the roof and yard sprinklers before they left and brought the animals with them. "That's really all we had time for."

"I know. And I'm sorry, but I'm still so scared."

"Mm hmm. We all are worried. Hopefully, they'll let us go back soon."

Mom's sister, who's been quiet this whole time, offers everyone some orange juice. "You know, you can stay here as long as you need to."

Dad stuffs his phone in his back pocket. "It looks like they've opened up Old Stagecoach, at least for people who live down there. What do you think, Val?"

"The kids could stay here while you guys go," Aunt Mary says after putting the orange juice back in the fridge.

"I want to go," Brindle says. *I have to go.* "Home is everything to me!"

Mom looks at Dad and he nods.

"Me too!" Willow shouts.

Taz looks at Mom and she puts her hands up as if to block the escalating commotion.

"Listen, Dad and I will go check it out to make sure it's safe for all of us to go back." She turns toward her sister and asks, "Are you sure it's okay for them to stay with you?"

Aunt Mary gives Taz a squeeze. "Of course. We'll have a good time."

"Dad?" *They've got to take me, too.* "Please!"

He puts his arm out for her and she slides underneath. Tears burn her eyes.

Mom hugs Willow and Taz and explains how it's better this way, that Brindle's older. "Who knows what we'll find."

Brindle's thoughts race from apocalyptic scenes and burned-down forests to their beautiful home in the canyon. *It has to still be there.*

She grabs a banana and cashews to take and fills her water bottle. Mom and Dad fill a backpack with supplies—just in case.

Dad says, "We may not be able to drive all the way there, so make sure you have decent walking shoes, okay?"

They shove stuff around in the Subaru to make room and slowly pull out of Aunt Mary's yard.

Half-an-hour later, after slowly driving down debris-littered streets, a highway patrol officer checks the address on Mom's driver's license. "Ma'am, no traffic is permitted beyond this park entrance. You'll either have to turn around here or there." He points to the next side road.

Mom sighs and drives the hundred feet farther. "Well, we could just walk, I suppose. What do you think?"

"Okay," Dad says hesitantly.

They pull over to park on the side of the road—about a mile from their dirt road. Evidently, there are downed trees blocking the road farther along.

This looks like a war zone. Brindle has never seen anything like it. Nobody is around and the place reeks of smoke and ash. She looks around at the trees that still stand, smoldering, among the burned brush surrounding them.

"Let's get our stuff," Dad says while Mom starts walking down the road. "You ready, Brindle?" He looks serious.

She nods, silently. Words don't feel appropriate. *What is happening?* She forces herself to put one foot in front of the other and follows her parents down the old paved road. She pulls the brim of her hat down over her eyebrows and slows. *Wait, isn't it usually shady here?* She looks up through the skeletal remains of the canopy.

"Look out for that branch, Brindle!" Dad calls.

She looks down just in time to walk around the obstacle.

Once on their dirt road, about a third of a mile in, Brindle peers through the eucalyptus grove at the new, unfinished house and it looks fine. She breathes a sigh of relief. Farther along, the neighborhood steer lies in the front yard of the ruins of a house, nonchalantly chewing his cud. *How can he look so unconcerned and just lie there, burping up old food and chewing it all over again?* Brindle stops alongside Dad and stares in disbelief at the pile of twisted metal and burnt appliances lying in heaps over the concrete slab. It stinks like nothing she's ever smelled before.

"Pretty awful," Dad mutters.

I can't respond.

A large tree trunk is lying across the road, blocking their way. *No one could drive back here, that's for sure.*

Brindle, Mom, and Dad duck through a barbed wire fence and wade through thick ash in the pasture. Brindle closes her mouth so she won't inhale as much floating, powdery silt.

The turn in the road brings the next property into focus. Their closest neighbor's house is a ramshackle cabin and still stands—amid the uncharred trees. She smiles at Dad, who's nodding at her. *Perhaps there's hope for ours then.*

The gate at the entrance to their place stands open, as they'd left it when they'd barreled down the road through clouds of smoke. *What will we find? Do we still have a house? Is our room—my books—the piano all still there?* Brindle follows behind Dad, almost too scared of what she might see. *The oak trees in front are still there and look good. Amazing!*

She inches forward, staring at the dirt in front of her tiny steps. Once she looks up—toward the house, there's no turning back. *As of right now, we haven't lost anything. And I hope we haven't. But if I look, and there's no house anymore, then it's all over. Everything is over!*

Brindle stops every few steps to take a breath and assess her lower surroundings. *Not yet. Just a little farther.* She hasn't allowed herself to look up. She assumes her parents are already there—at the house. *Yes, at our house and everything is still the same.* She keeps trying to convince herself it's all going to be okay.

And finally, she can't help it, she looks up. She has to take a few more steps and then peers around the huge boulder. There it is.... Only, it's not. She shuts her eyes tightly before opening them again to make sure what she saw is real. *Is it? Is it really gone?* The old rock chimney stands precariously over the crumbled foundation. She stares at the twisted iron bed frames, the scorched refrigerator lying on its side, the cast iron stove—cracked and misshapen, and broken glass everywhere. The stench overwhelms her. She turns away, pulling her shirt up over her nose, and notices flowers blooming beside her. *Huh? How can that be?*

Her eyes sting and she coughs. Dad comes over and puts his arm around her. That's when she loses it. She cries hard into his chest and he wraps his arms around her. She feels as if she's lost everything: their house, her books, her natural sanctuary here in the canyon they call home. Brindle buries herself into Dad's strong embrace and sobs. She wobbles, unsteady on her feet, as if she's going to faint as her own voice wails, unrecognizable.

How can I possibly go on? A lot of good my praying did. She slides down into the ashes, next to their demolished house, and sinks into oblivion. *At least that's what it feels like. What's left anymore?* Dad sits beside her and points to the flowers she noticed earlier.

"So what," she mumbles. "It doesn't matter. Nothing matters anymore." She picks one of the small purple flowers and twirls the stem between her fingers.

Dad slowly walks back to Mom, leaving Brindle alone with her thoughts.

Sometime later, she hears voices coming up the dirt road.

"It sounds like Willow and Taz," Dad says. "What are they doing here?"

Aunt Mary appears from behind the boulder with Willow and Taz on each side of her. She stops suddenly and gasps, bringing both hands up to her face. "Oh, my gosh!"

Willow and Taz stand there stunned.

"Mary?" Mom says from the other side of the smoking debris. "What—" She strides over to envelop her children in a hug as Dad pulls Brindle up to join them.

Aunt Mary wraps her arms across her chest. "I'm so sorry. This is awful."

Dad gets down on his knee to face the kids. "I know this looks bad, but—"

Aunt Mary interrupts. "I didn't plan on bringing them, but they kept insisting and crying. I didn't know what else to do."

"It's okay," Mom says. "Maybe it's for the best."

"Hey, guys?" Dad says, standing up. "We'll be okay. You do know that, right?"

Willow and Taz both nod, and Brindle does, too.

I really want to believe him.

Mom says, "We're all okay. The animals are okay. We're safe now." She leads Willow and Taz toward the smoldering remains, but turns back to her sister. "It's all right, Mary. You did the right thing."

The group carefully makes its way around the piles of debris lying within and spilling over the crumbled foundation walls. The rock chimney towers in the middle of the ravaged site; the wood-burning stove lies on its side, discolored and warped; the antique iron bed frames from Brindle and Willow's room upstairs wrap around the tipped-over carcass of the refrigerator like a spider. And it stinks, like something beyond awful.

"I need to pee," Taz whines, wiggling uncomfortably.

Mom raises her eyebrows at Brindle.

Brindle nods. She wants an escape anyway. They walk down the dirt path into the creek bed toward a stump poking up in a sea of ashes.

"This place looks like some other world from 'Star Wars,' huh?"

"Yeah." Taz unzips his pants and a yellow stream reaches the blackened remains of the oak tree. Immediately, smoke rises and the surface sizzles. Taz gasps, but then laughs. "Wow! That's awesome! Look at that!"

Brindle can't help, but laugh, too. But then, Willow screams nearby.

"Ouch! Ow, ow, ow!" She starts crying, hopping toward the dirt road.

Mom, Dad, and Aunt Mary run down to see what's wrong as Willow sits in the dirt, pulling off her sandal. "Oohh, it hurts!"

Brindle looks down at her sister's bare foot and sees a huge blister—bright red. Mom takes one look and hurries over to the rock planter to cut a leaf of Aloe vera that happened to survive the firestorm. She returns, skinning it with the pocket knife she usually carries, and gently presses it onto the wound—against Willow's wishes, and gradually Willow grows quiet.

"Does it feel better now?" Mom asks.

Willow nods and wipes the tears with the back of her dirty hand, leaving brown smears across her cheeks.

"Shall I pick some more?" Dad asks.

"Mm hmm," Mom says. "To take back with us."

"We'd better get going," Dad says. "It'll be dark soon and we don't have flashlights. Come on, Willow. Climb aboard."

Brindle helps her sister onto Dad's back while Mom and Aunt Mary gather the backpacks and waters they had come with.

Brindle and her family start walking back out the road. She notices a tree up the mountain, barely standing, with small flames periodically wrapping around the trunk. She points it out.

"Should we do something about that?"

"No." Mom stops to look. "It wouldn't do any good, anyway."

The group continues on in silence and Brindle turns inward. That same feeling of foreboding comes over her and she remembers being pinned to the ocean floor. And that same voice pierces through. *Everything is going to change. The belief in having control is an illusion.*

Something else bad is going to happen? No! I can't take any more.

6

ALL TOGETHER NOW

Paige

Pick yourself up after a fall and dance on.

Paige reaches into her backpack and pulls out the spiral notebook labeled, *Social Studies*, as the bell rings and the short, round teacher closes the door.

"All right, class, today we're going to talk about history in the making. Right now—every day." She starts practically every day like this.

A boy in the back raises his hand and asks, "Do we have to take notes on this?"

"That's your call," she answers matter-of-factly, before asking the loaded question. "How many of you have been sexually harassed?" She scans the room with a serious look as eyes nervously dart back and forth.

A few boys giggle in the corner of the room.

"This is no laughing matter!" she snaps. "You ought to be ashamed of yourselves."

Eventually, three girls reluctantly raise their hands.

Wow, they're brave. I don't know if I could do that.

The teacher continues. "Recent statistics show that perhaps half the population, including males, has experienced some sort of sexual harassment." She scans the expectant faces in her audience. "We're not only talking about rape. It's any behavior characterized by the making of unwelcome and inappropriate sexual remarks or physical advances—cat calls, lewd motions, invading another's space in a threatening way."

Silence takes over the room.

Paige can think of multiple times when boys brushed up against her in the hallways of middle school. *Sure, the halls were crowded, but they didn't have to do that.* The teacher's voice interrupts her thoughts.

"It's everywhere and it happens all the time. In fact, bullying can be a form of it." She pauses again. "How many of you have heard of the *Me Too Movement?*"

This time, most of the hands in the room drift upward.

"Can someone please tell us what the *Me Too Movement* is about?"

Paige finds herself speaking. "Didn't it start to help survivors of sexual violence, especially young women—" she stops.

The teacher nods.

"And now, women from all over seem to be joining in?"

"Yes. The hope is that, if everyone is more aware of sexual harassment, tolerance for it will decrease. And the *Me Too Movement* is an effort to effect social change. Primarily, it's been through social media. But the point is to increase awareness of this absolutely unacceptable behavior." She slowly walks around the quiet room, her low heels clicking ominously on the hard floor.

Another girl raises her hand and the teacher nods to her.

"Doesn't it also have to do with body image, like you deserve to be happy in whatever body shape you have?"

"Somewhat. It has helped people begin to feel a little braver to come forward with the hope to dissipate the power, patriarchy, and oppression so many of us face—particularly women." She continues walking. "It's all tied together in what healthy relationships really are and how important consent is when dealing with another person. Is it okay with you for them to do whatever it is to you? If not—say no. And no means no!" She stops in the middle of the room and turns around slowly. "Class? Consent is a fundamental concept that has relevance for all ages."

Paige really likes this teacher, but is also a little nervous around her. But one thing's for sure—she brings the topic to life in a way most of them will probably remember for a long, long time.

A small town like ours is probably pretty lucky to have someone like her teaching in our school. She always gives me things to think about.

After school, Paige makes her way out through the crowded quad and overhears a group of girls talking about *her* friend.

"I can't believe that girl, Randi—she's dating *him*!"

"I know, huh? Did you see them at lunch today? Holding hands and everything."

What? Paige hurries past them, not wanting to hear any more about their racial biases. *So Neanderthal. Anyway, they're just friends, but even so, it shouldn't matter.*

Later, at the studio, Paige ponders the suggestions from her new doctor, a naturopath. Changing what she eats won't be easy. *But it's worth it if it works.* Gluten-free, dairy-free, and lots of water—*that part's easy.* She hasn't been able to eat *normally* for weeks. Almost everything bothers her stomach and sends her running to the bathroom, or at least makes her cramp. She's practically living on fruit lately.

She gets up to take her banana peel to the trash and Miss Val looks up.

"Good choice for a snack, Paige."

"Yeah, I guess it is. At least my stomach agrees."

"Are you feeling any better? I know it's been frustrating. Sometimes food can make a big difference in how we feel. I know it does for me, anyway."

"Do you still drink your green smoothies?" Paige has seen her with those often over the last couple years.

"Yes." Miss Val lifts a container filled with green juice and sets it back down. "Packed full of garden greens, except this one was store-bought since we don't have a garden anymore."

Paige then remembers her manners. "I'm so sorry about your house. It must be awful."

Miss Val nods and turns back to her choreography notebook.

She looks sad. Paige walks back to the group clustered under the ballet *barres*, stretching and talking about the fire. When she'd first arrived, lots of parents were gathered around Miss Val, offering their condolences to both her and Brindle for losing practically everything in the fire. *It must be so hard for them.*

"Yeah, the only thing left was our rickety rock chimney. And the smell—it's awful," Brindle says while sitting on the floor holding her feet and wiggling her knees up and down, doing the butterfly.

"Like what kind of smell?" Sophia asks from her pancake straddle. "Like something rotten or what?"

They all stare at Brindle expectantly.

"No, not really." She pauses mid-butterfly and makes a face. "Kind of a cross between burned plastic and something dead—" She furrows her eyebrows as if trying to find the right words. "Really bad farts, I guess."

They can't help it. Everyone laughs. But then they stop short.

She just lost everything. It's really not funny at all. "Where are you staying, Brindle?" *I try to steer the conversation in another direction so she doesn't fall apart in front of everyone.*

"We're camped out at my aunt's house for now. Hopefully, we'll figure out something else soon—"

Brindle is interrupted when Miss Val asks them to put the *barres* out so they can begin. Jack takes one and Paige grabs one end of another to help Todd carry it.

"I know our whole *Nutcracker* schedule got blown out of whack, so we'll have to work extra hard to make up for lost time. As you all know, many people lost their homes in this fire, including us. Luckily, I did save my choreography notebook, so at least we don't have to recreate everything from scratch." Miss Val takes a deep breath and blows out.

I'll bet she's more upset than she's letting on.

The dancers stare at her for an uncomfortable moment of silence. *Did she lose her train of thought?*

Then she shakes her head. "*Pliés* now." Miss Val moves to the front of the center *barre* and demonstrates the first exercise.

After the class has finished the *pliés, tendus, dégagés, ronde de jambs, frappés,* and *grand battements,* the students carry the *barres* back to the wall and stretch in the center. Their teacher pulls over a chair to sit in front.

"Okay, everybody, you know the drill. Not everyone gets the part they want and I need you to be good sports about it. I have to look at the big picture and assign roles accordingly. Are you ready?" She looks at them and raises her eyebrows.

"Of course," Paige says, wiggling her hands excitedly. "We're all atwitter."

The class giggles.

"Like being twitterpated?" Randi asks, leaning back onto Todd's outstretched leg.

"Aahh, ain't that cute," Jack teases and Todd's face breaks into a big smile.

"Yeah." Last spring, she'd had to explain how she'd learned it from *Winnie the Pooh* and that it meant something like waking up to the joys of spring. Paige's smile slowly fades as she begins to put one-plus-one together. *Why didn't I see it before? That's why Randi's been too busy to hang out with me as often. They really are together! Shouldn't I be happy for them? What kind of friend am I and why do I feel so let down?*

"Oh," Miss Val begins. "There's one important thing we should probably discuss first. I'm going to need extra help from you, and your parents, to rebuild some of the props for *The Nutcracker*. The fire burned them because they were stored in our barn."

The group gasps.

"All of them?" Deanne asks.

"No, but some of them. Would you all be able to help out with that? And ask your parents as well, okay?"

"Of course," Jack answers. "I can stay and help after some of the Saturday rehearsals."

"Me, too," Paige says, trying to regain her usual good mood.

Randi looks around at everyone. "We'll do whatever it takes, right?" They all nod in agreement.

"All right! You're so awesome. Did everyone get the latest Dancespiration—about rising up after a fall?"

"I did," Paige answers. "How fitting for these days, huh?"

"It turns out that, yes, it is. But it's too bad the fire came in the *Nutcracker* year." Miss Val folds her hands together and nods graciously to the dancers scattered around the floor. "Most of you will have dual roles since there are two acts in our story. Randi will be the Sugar Plum Fairy in Act Two and Mrs. Stahlbaum in Act One."

Randi tucks up her knees and does a double spin on her rear, giggling and clapping her hands excitedly.

Paige leans over and teases, "Gee, you don't look happy at all."

"Yippee! Yes I am!" she loudly whispers back.

"Deanne, you'll play Clara."

Deanne quickly nods and grins at Brindle and Sophia.

Miss Val smiles. "And Jack, you'll be Dr. Stahlbaum and the Cavalier."

"Woo hoo—big man!" Todd jokes and the rest of them join in his laughter, including Miss Val.

"Okay now, let's keep it together." She smiles warmly and points to Todd. "And here we have the Nutcracker!"

"Me?" Todd shouts and everybody cracks up.

"Of course," Miss Val says. "Who else?"

Todd stands and marches stiffly around in place like a soldier, which encourages further teasing.

Miss Val puts her hands up and grins. "May I continue?"

The class quiets down and faces her expectantly once again.

"The rest of you will be party guests in Act One as well as dancers in the Waltz of the Flowers in Act Two. And Paige? You'll be our ballerina doll."

"Really?" Paige trembles with excitement. *Wow, a real solo! I guess this is my last chance for* The Nutcracker *since I'll be off at college the next time they do this in two years.*

Miss Val nods. "Oh, and Jack told me that his friend Mike, from the drama department at school, has agreed to be the crazy toy maker, Drosselmeyer. Isn't that right?"

"Yeah," Jack says, cracking his neck to the side. "He says he just has to get through the play they're working on now."

Miss Val looks down at her notes and smiles. "Splendid."

"How about the little kids? Who are they going to be?" Paige asks.

"Well, the Beginning and Intermediate ballet will be the party guests' children in Act One, and the Intermediates will also be snowflakes in Act Two. As far as the gymnasts go, the preschoolers will be the squirrels who come out from under Mother Ginger's enormous skirt."

"Squirrels?" asks Julie, the new girl.

"Oh." Miss Val chuckles. "Well, what is the original nutcracker, anyway?" She waits for a response.

"Squirrels!" Todd yells.

"*Ardillas!*" Sophia adds.

"Of course they are." Miss Val laughs. "It's our own version. It does seem fitting, doesn't it?"

Julie smiles and her cheeks dimple cutely. "Yeah, I guess it does."

"Anyway," she continues. "JP, my gymnastics assistant, will be helping out, as usual. The Intermediate gymnasts will be the Chinese dancers and the rats, that's what we call them." She laughs again. Miss Val takes the liberty to change the villain characters to rats instead of mice. "And the soldiers will be the Advanced gymnasts, while the Russian dancers and candy canes, those will be other classes, like tap, hip hop—" She pauses. "The Spanish dancers will probably be the local Folklorico group."

Deanne raises her hand. "Could I be an Arabian dancer, too?"

"Not and be Clara at the same time," Miss Val explains. "Besides, we like to have the belly dancers come take part in our performance for that. Okay, up and at 'em!"

Paige stands up, practices a *pirouette,* and asks, "Are we going to start rehearsing today?"

Miss Val carries the chair back to the desk and answers. "Yes, we most certainly are."

She looks a little livelier now than before class began. Maybe teaching is what she needs to get through such a huge loss.

"Since we're all here now, we'll start learning the party scene at the opening of the ballet. For you who have solo parts or are in smaller group numbers, I'll set up separate rehearsal times to teach those dances. Now, let's figure out where each of you will begin!"

For the remainder of the class time, the group walks through the procession of the guests arriving at the Christmas party, greeted by Dr. and Mrs. Stahlbaum. Miss Val points to where the young children will be and explains to Deanne, as Clara, how she, and Fritz, her little brother in the story, are to interact with them.

She says Fritz will be one of the boys from Intermediate ballet. Even though Miss Val worked all this out in advance, it still needs to be blocked out with proper timing and spacing.

Paige is happy for the distraction from her best friend's new relationship, and her own stomach issues, as well as all the concerns of the fire's aftermath. She knows everything is far from being settled, but at least one thing, her ballet family, is intact and working together again.

7

ALTERNATE DIGS

Brindle

The beauty of dance comes from within.

Dad steers the Subaru around a bicyclist and turns into a short driveway. "There it is. It may not be much, but it ought to suffice, at least for a while."

Straight ahead sits a little blue house, not far from a big blue house.

"At least it's not an apartment," Mom says, turning around to address Brindle and her two siblings in the backseat.

After they park in front of the smaller house, Willow leans forward between the bucket seats. "I thought you meant the bigger house. We're not gonna fit all our stuff in there."

"Well, Willow," Dad says. "We don't have much stuff anymore."

"That's for sure," Mom mumbles and they all get out of the car and walk to the front door of what, apparently, will be their home for the foreseeable future.

Brindle can't think of anything to say. She's in a daze and has been since they first witnessed the remains of their beloved homestead. Her body moves on autopilot, trailing her family into the unfamiliar place Mom and Dad leased after living at her aunt's for almost a month. *Will anything ever be normal again?*

The kitchen is not much more than a hallway. A dining table occupies one end of the open living room and a couch is set against the opposite wall under a picture window. There are only two bedrooms, each furnished with a double bed, dresser, and side tables.

Brindle likes her privacy and would love her own bed again, even her own room, but it looks like she'll still be sharing with Willow. "Does it come with this furniture?"

Mom answers, "Yes, that's why we chose it, and because it's a house and *not* an apartment. We just couldn't see ourselves living in the middle of town with streetlights and sirens, you know?"

That's for sure. Even amid all this upheaval in their lives, that is one thing Brindle remains very clear on. She needs nature around her and space to wander.

Dad pulls the cushions off the sofa and opens it into a bed.

"That's cool!" Taz shouts. "Can I sleep here?"

"Why, yes you can, bud!" He grins.

Brindle goes out the back door and walks over to an old swing set. *Mom's right, at least it's got a yard.* She watches a car go by and pull into a neighboring property. Willow's and Taz's whooping and hollering carries out on the breeze as they run through the house. *At least they're excited.* She settles tentatively onto the board seat of a swing and gently pushes her weight back and forth with her toes on the ground. Her eyes settle on a tree in the distance when she hears the cawing of a crow. *I guess it's sort of peaceful here.* But then a motorcycle speeds by and disrupts her temporary calm.

The following day, Sunday, Brindle gets startled awake by the guinea pig's loud squeaking. The rodent has been living with all three of them in the shared bedroom at Aunt Mary's house. *I wish I had my own room.*

"Taz! Get up and feed Tiger. She won't be quiet!"

Her little brother squirms sleepily out of his bedroll and staggers over to his pet's cage. Willow bounds out of bed, bouncing Brindle around uncomfortably, and leaves the room. *I certainly won't miss this if I ever get my own bed again.*

Today is the day they are moving into the rental house, so Brindle rolls out of bed, sorts through a few hand-me-down clothes in a box, and gets dressed. They don't actually have much, so it's a good thing the place comes furnished. The horses and goats will stay at Aunt Mary's. This afternoon, after dropping things off at the rental, they're all going down the hill, as everyone in Nuevo says, toward San Diego. There's a church warehousing donations for fire victims— mostly clothes and accessories.

The little blue house isn't really all that bad. Besides, it's temporary. Brindle folds and arranges her shirts, pants, and underwear into the drawers on her side of the bed while Willow haphazardly shoves hers into the other dresser. Mom is clanging around in the kitchen putting away the groceries they'd picked up on the way over.

Taz pokes his head in the doorway and the two cats, Bonnie and Clyde, squeeze by. "You guys gotta see my bed. There's a dinosaur on it!"

"Whatever," Willow responds, but follows him out anyway.

Sure enough, there really is a dinosaur there. Brindle manages a giggle at the oversized, green brontosaurus perched on the back of the living room sofa. *At least he gets his own bed. No wonder he's excited.*

Dad says, "What do you think, bud?"

"It's so awesome!" Taz answers.

Bonnie jumps onto the back of the couch, taking ownership as she licks her yellow stripes. Nutkins pokes his head in the doorway, which causes the black fur on Clyde's back to rise before he bolts into Mom and Dad's room.

Willow laughs, but then complains, "I'm starving. Can we go soon?"

"Me too. I'm dying for a bird dog." Dad loves bean and cheese burritos and has his own name for them.

Brindle's stomach growls.

"Okay, Mexican food it is. Let's go! We'll go through the drive-through on the way to get our new wardrobes," Mom says.

As they get into the Subaru, Taz asks, "Hey, Brindle, what are you gonna get?"

"A bean burrito, of course. And, let me guess. You want your usual quesadilla, right?" *He's so predictable—as am I, I suppose.*

Heaps of clothes cover the tables in the huge room. Mom shows her FEMA card to a lady sitting at the check-in desk, proving they are fire victims. Brindle follows along, dazed.

There's so much stuff here. Her mind wanders aimlessly as she picks up a shirt here—and puts it down, and a jacket there—and puts it down. *I just want my own clothes back.* They were comfortable and familiar. She hates shopping and even though this isn't exactly shopping, it kind of feels like it. The familiar glazed-over sensation creeps in as she drifts from one pile to the next.

Meanwhile, Willow is bopping along with Dad and Taz, picking out things to wear and tossing them into the cart. Mom comes back to help Brindle find some suitable attire for her daily life.

What will daily life even look like? She's home most of the time these days anyway, except for ballet and the library, since she home-schools now. With this in mind, she finds a pair of grey sweatpants, a few earth-tone T-shirts, and a couple pairs of faded blue jeans. *It's a start.*

An hour-and-a-half later, the car is packed solid with bedding, clothing for the entire family, towels, and other necessities. Brindle just wants to start rebuilding their home, like they've talked about. Find an architect, discuss plans, and break ground. *Let's just hurry up. Another log cabin might be nice.* The canyon calls to her, like a long lost friend. It hasn't been *that* long, but she feels pulled in unfamiliar ways. *Even if I didn't know it before, I'm absolutely sure now—I belong in that place. We have to get back there soon or I'll go crazy.*

Once they return, Deanne shows up just in time to help Brindle organize her new things. "Okay, show me what you got. Did they have any cute clothes there?"

Brindle hands her a large bag and grabs a box full of dishes from the back of the car. "I don't know. Lots of stuff, that's for sure." She sets down the box on the kitchen counter and points the way to the small bedroom she'll be sharing with Willow.

Deanne sets the bag on the bed and looks around the room. "Not bad. It's kind of cute."

"I don't even have my own bed anymore," Brindle says, grumpily.

"Well, I guess you could look at it as having an ongoing slumber party with your sister." Deanne laughs.

"Well, there's that," Brindle says, rolling her eyes. "Thanks for coming over to help. I just can't seem to get very enthused about any of this."

Deanne pats Brindle on the head—like a big sister might do, except they're the same age. She dumps out the contents from the bag and arranges them into separate piles. "What? Nothing cute? Nothing fun?"

Mom walks in and presents a pretty blue blouse on a hanger. "This looks a bit young for me. How about you try it on, Brindle?"

Deanne takes the garment from her and holds it up to Brindle. "It'll bring out the blue in your eyes. Nice pick, Miss Val."

"Yeah, okay," Brindle says, taking all the clothes and cramming them back into the bag. "Off to the washing machine with these."

Willow comes in bouncing a big, red rubber ball and flops down on the bed.

"Hi Willow," Deanne says, then follows Brindle to the back porch to put in the laundry.

Nutkins follows the two girls out to the swings while they wait for the wash to finish. Brindle scoops his front paws onto her lap and hugs him like a person.

"You know what? I'm going to take you shopping. Every girl needs at least one killer outfit she can feel like a million bucks in. What do you say?"

Brindle finds herself agreeing, even though it's not one of her favorite activities. She's just grateful to not have to deal with all this by herself right now. "Thanks, Deanne."

Later that night, Brindle finds herself uncovered and yanks the blanket from Willow's side. Thunder shakes the dresser mirror, yet her sister continues her little mouse snores, unaffected. *I wish I could sleep like that.* In the next room, she hears snippets of a conversation.

"I don't know if I have it in me to rebuild." A rumble cuts off Mom's voice.

Blinding light streaks through the room, and Brindle jolts upright. She glances around the now darkened space.

Dad's muffled voice permeates the thin walls of the temporary rental. "Well, what if we—" Again, silenced by another round of loud claps and sudden light.

What are they talking about? She tiptoes across the floor to listen, her ear against the separating wall.

"Maybe we should just sell," Mom says.

Oh no! We can't do that. It's home. The canyon is our real home, not the house. Don't they know that?

Hail crashes down in rapid *staccato* beats on the tin roof, shutting out any more eavesdropping on their private conversation. Her mind reels with thoughts of condo living with sirens piercing the nights, exhaust fumes drifting into open windows, pavement covering up once fertile ground, and people everywhere—with no privacy or silent refuge. She runs back to the bed and clings tightly to her pillow. And then the tears come, and the sniffles, and the shoulder-heaving sobs. She cries into the covers so no one hears. After a while, the horrid sobbing subsides, but with no letup of tears. She leaves the bedroom and goes out the back door of the house. The hail has stopped. Nutkins is there on the back porch and gets up to greet her. Brindle crumples onto the slab and leans against the wall, crying freely now. The dog licks her face, whining. *He understands.*

"You want to go home, too, don't you boy?"

She wraps her arms around her good friend and he leans into her and slowly lies down on her lap.

"I love you, Nutkins. We *have* to convince them to move back home. And build a new house. Or live in a cave. It doesn't matter what we live in, even a tent, just as long as we go back home."

She stares out at the backyard, now that the thunder has stopped, and thinks of Dorothy in *The Wizard of Oz*. "There's no place like home. There's no place like home," she repeats.

This can't be happening. The possibility of not having her favorite place in the whole wide world to retreat to, especially in times like this, is unbearable. The tears return with a vengeance and she hugs her whimpering companion and rocks back and forth in the only movement she can muster. *Am I going insane?*

8

CALMING THE GUT

Paige

Visualize perfect balance then make it so.

A bell jingles when Paige closes the door leading into the naturopath's office. *This doesn't look like a doctor's office. It's more like a small living room.* A dark blue sofa sits underneath the large bay window and bookshelves line the opposite wall. A young woman sitting behind the desk in the corner invites them over. While Mom checks her in, Paige peruses some of the titles on the shelf: *Clean, Vegan for Everybody, The Gluten-Free Bible* ... Just as she sits down, a middle-aged woman in a flowered skirt appears in the doorway and says her name softly.

"Paige? You and your mom may come back now, if you'd like."

They follow her into a smaller room with a massage table, a petite mahogany desk, and a couple of comfy chairs.

"Have a seat." The nice woman gestures toward the chairs and then joins them. "I'm Dr. Johnson."

The lamp on the desk illuminates a potted plant with soft light as more rays stream in from the open window. Paige stares out at the yellow flowers dancing between the blades of green grass in the shade under the tree.

"So, Paige. Do you know what a naturopath does?"

Paige looks at Mom and then back to the pretty doctor. "Treat things with more natural remedies?"

"Yes." She smiles warmly. "We try to look at you as a whole person and not just at your symptoms. After all, everything is connected and can't operate on its own. So, we already spoke on the phone and I'd suggested to try going both gluten- and dairy-free. Can you tell me how that's going?"

Paige does her best to explain how practically every time she eats her insides rebel and don't cooperate. And she's noticed that things are slightly better when she avoids bread and milk. It's only been a week.

"How long has this been going on?"

"A couple months." Paige watches Dr. Johnson's expressions as she talks. *This is different from those other doctors. I don't feel rushed and she's really listening.*

After Dr. Johnson hears her story, she nods sympathetically. "Your blood panel came back showing gluten and dairy sensitivities. That's probably why you feel worse after you eat foods with wheat or milk. It's not that uncommon these days, especially here in the U.S., where gluten is added to so many things. A lot of us have simply had too much of it. Our bodies are yelling, 'Enough already!'" She chuckles softly and smiles.

The doctor asks Paige to lie on the table and pull her shirt up over her belly. As she gently palpates her abdomen, she talks about making different choices concerning food. "And the decisions we make about that, and everything really, directly affect our state of being, and of course, our health."

Once Paige and Dr. Johnson are sitting back in the chairs, she hands her a list of some books she and Mom can read, along with some helpful websites. By the time they leave, Paige senses a lightness in her step she hasn't felt in a while.

"I guess I may not be terminal after all. At least not yet." She giggles and Mom joins in.

"Of course not, you silly goose!"

"Maybe I *can* actually start feeling better."

"Well then, we'd better get home and order those books right away. But first, let's swing by the grocery store and see what more we can find that's both gluten and dairy-free."

"Sounds good to me," Paige says, slipping into the passenger seat of the car as the sun sinks behind the mountain.

Another thing the naturopath had mentioned was how the overuse of antibiotics has severely cut down the number of *good bacteria* in our digestive systems.

And many people have what is called "leaky gut syndrome." Paige doesn't quite understand all this yet, but she's trying.

Evidently, fermented foods, like sauerkraut and pickles, can help rebuild "the gut flora," as the doctor put it. She also recommended Paige start taking probiotics—so they'll search the store for those, as well.

The next day, Paige studies some tiny wiggly creatures swimming under the lens of her microscope in the high school science lab, then pulls her eye away to sketch a replica of them in her lab book. Then she returns her focus to the miniscule life in front of her. *Is this what those gut microbes Dr. Johnson talked about look like? Maybe, later at home, I'll look online and see.* Science has always interested her, and now she senses a more personal reason to do more research.

After school, ballet class is in full swing. Deanne, as Clara, practices her big sister role with little brother, Fritz, for the first time. Miss Val has her hands full trying to get him to interact with Clara in a more dramatic way. *He looks kind of shy.* They play tug-of-war with a wooden nutcracker doll, and so far anyway, it doesn't look very convincing. Randi and Jack are practicing what they know of their duet as the Sugar Plum Fairy and the Cavalier. Paige is still trying to memorize her beginning steps in the *Waltz of the Flowers.*

Miss Val walks over to the stereo. "All right dancers, places for Act One!" She reminds each of them where they need to be in the beginning. "Clara and Fritz, look excited and point at the tree! Randi and Jack? Remember, you are hosting this festive occasion and must greet guests enthusiastically as they enter. Okay, Paige and Brindle, you come on first and you'll have, I think, three Beginners and two Intermediate children with you. And remember to usher them over to the tree after you greet Dr. and Mrs. Stahlbaum, okay?"

The Advanced group walks through the opening scene without music. This is the way Miss Val teaches them their dances, counting out the phrases before practicing with accompaniment. When they are all onstage, the movements combine dancing and acting.

It's just beginning to feel like we're in that other world, on Christmas Eve.

Later, Miss Val calls over the music, "Remember the variable phrasing here!"

Toward the end of class, they rehearse the March Dance, Paige's favorite. Brindle walks forward on her right, behind Jack and Randi. Their inside arms are extended forward, with the person on the right's hand (Brindle's) resting on top of hers.

It's all so regal, and formal. The music makes it come alive.

When Miss Val calls an end to class, Paige sits under the *barres* to remove her *pointe* shoes and notices one of the books she saw at the naturopath's office laying on top of Brindle's ballet bag.

"Are you reading that?" Paige asks.

"Yeah, well, kind of. It's more like a recipe book, but there's some other information in there, too." Brindle sits down and hands the book to her.

"What do you think of it? I mean, are there any good recipes in it?" Paige flips through the pages of the vegan cookbook. "Cashew cheese?"

"Yeah, it's delicious. I've made it twice and it's good on almost everything." Brindle smiles, engaging in the topic. "I could make you some to try, if you'd like."

Paige nods. "Sure." She looks at a few more pictures of brightly colored vegetable dishes and hands the book back. "I'm trying to eat more gluten and dairy-free these days." She tells Brindle a little about the naturopath she's seeing and the stomach issues they're trying to address.

"You are what you eat. At least, that's what they say, right? It's part of the reason I became vegan. That, and because I also want to try to eat more responsibly." Brindle tucks the book into her bag and stands up to leave.

"Maybe we should cook together sometime. What do you think? It's hard trying to figure this stuff out on my own. My mom is trying, too, but I don't really know anyone else who eats like this, you know?" Paige slips her arm through the long strap and heaves her satchel of ballet supplies up onto her shoulder.

"I know. Tell me about it."

"Come on, Brindle. Sophia's mom is here. We gotta go," Deanne says, poking her in the arm.

"Okay, okay." Brindle turns back to Paige. "Yeah, let's get together."

After Paige has spent an hour-and-a-half on her math homework, her stomach rumbles and the mouth-watering thought of a giant chocolate chip cookie distills in her mind. *Oh, the chewy, rich goodness of that delicious morsel. How I long for thee.* Mom's in the kitchen tossing a salad and Paige strolls by and snags a piece of lettuce. *It's just not the same.*

"Is Dad coming down this weekend? It's been a few months since I've seen him."

"Didn't he say he was busy the next few weeks?" Mom sets the bowl of salad on the table and goes to the stove to stir a pan of something.

"What? He didn't tell me that," Paige says. "It's like he doesn't have time for me anymore. What gives?"

"I don't know, sweetie. I'm just the middle man here."

"I miss him and I don't understand why he's doing this to me. It hurts my feelings that he can't even take the time to come see his younger daughter." Tears sting Paige's eyes, so she turns and blinks them away before Mom can see.

It's a little late for that and Mom comes over and hugs her tightly. "But, you know, I love you so much." She pulls back and massages Paige's shoulders. "He just doesn't know what he's missing."

"Thanks, Mom. But it still hurts."

"I know it does. Maybe you could give him a call later, if you'd like."

"Yeah, maybe."

The two of them set the table and sit down to their dinner of boiled zucchini over rice and salad. It may not be that exciting, but hopefully Paige's insides will not rebel with this cuisine. That giant chocolate chip cookie drifts into her consciousness again and she fights hard against the image. *Go away!* But it lingers anyway, through the next hour of homework, the teeth brushing, and the packing of tomorrow's lunch, and then snuggles into bed with her.

Trying hard to banish the tempting demon, she finds herself humming the tune from the March Dance. She closes her eyes and visualizes herself doing the steps to the music with Brindle as her partner. Miss Val often tells them to do this when they go to bed. It can help to internalize the dance. *Sometimes I'm lucky and it comes in my dreams. And if I'm* really *lucky, I'm the star of the show.* She laughs at the thought. *As if* that *would ever happen.*

9

Finding Commonalities

Brindle

A successful pas de deux requires both dancers to be at their best. You owe it to yourself, and to your partner.

The three musketeers and Deanne's mother walk across the mall to Forever 21, where Deanne insists Brindle will find the perfect outfit.

"This is really nice of you to do this for me," Brindle says.

"Oh, it's our pleasure. It's the least we can do. You've all been through so much and it's good to be able to help in any way we can." Deanne's mom ushers the girls into the store and tells them she'll be back in a few minutes. "I have to make a phone call."

Sophia pulls Brindle by the arm, following Deanne toward the back.

"Ooh, this one is pretty nice," Deanne says.

"No, wrong color," Sophia warns. "How about this one?"

"Mm, no."

Brindle observes her two friends dance excitedly from rack to rack, as if each one has better offerings. *How do they get so excited about this? I hope there is something made of cotton.*

Sophia holds up a pair of jeans and asks if they're the right size.

"I don't know." Brindle holds them to her lap to assess.

"Don't you know what size you wear?" Deanne asks incredulously.

A clerk joins them. "How about these? They might be closer to her size."

Brindle shakes her head. "Do you have any regular blue jeans?"

The clerk stares at her and then glances toward Deanne and Sophia. "This way."

They follow her to another rack and watch her rifle through varying shades of blue. "What about this?" She smiles and hands Brindle a cute jean skirt.

It's actually not bad. Brindle takes it and starts toward the dressing rooms.

"Not yet," Deanne says. "Let's look for a top to go with it."

The clerk leaves to assist another customer and they're left on their own again. For the next ten minutes, though it feels much longer to Brindle, Sophia and Deanne select things to try on themselves.

Deanne's mom comes back into the store and finds Brindle standing by herself with the skirt draped over her arm. "Did you find something, Brindle?"

"I'll try this on and see."

"How about a blouse? Let's see what we can find, shall we?"

Deanne and Sophia return with several colorful outfits to try on, and three tops for Brindle.

"Those look nice. I think any of them could work for you," Deanne's mother suggests.

All three girls crowd into the largest of the dressing rooms and the flurry of garment changing begins. The skirt and the third top suit Brindle just fine, and they are actually more comfortable than she expected.

"*Anaranjada, verdad?*" Brindle admires her orange top with the word *BREATHE* written in rope-like letters across the front.

"*Sí, una camisa anaranjada,*" Sophia says.

"This is actually kind of fun, you guys."

"It is," Sophia says.

Deanne laughs and wiggles into a pair of skinny jeans.

They decide to wear their new outfits home and convince Deanne's mom to let them go get ice cream while she runs an errand. She says she'll pick them up at the north entrance in an hour. They giggle and make their way through the busy mall.

Who would have thought I'd actually have fun doing this? Sometimes I even surprise myself. Brindle smiles at her two friends, grateful for their loyalty to her. "I suppose I can be a stick-in-the-mud sometimes, huh?"

"Ha ha," Deanne laughs.

Sophia adds, "We love you anyway."

Brindle flips over one more time and throws off the covers. The alarm clock beside the bed blinks 1:03 a.m. and she lets out an exasperated huff. *Not again.* Every night, and sometimes during the day, too, visions of the fire rampage through her brain, scorching new territory and eroding any peace she may have gained. Usually, she feels so even tempered. *Not anymore!* She takes the notebook off her nightstand and pads into the kitchen, where she won't disturb Willow.

A scuffling sound is coming from the corner of the living room and she pauses to listen. *Oh, it's Taz's guinea pig. Doesn't Tiger ever sleep?* She unfolds a tri-fold project board and sets it on the dining table to keep the light from waking her little brother. Mom had bought it so if any of them needed to do something in the kitchen while Taz was asleep on the living room couch, they wouldn't disturb him as much.

She pours herself some filtered water from the pitcher in the refrigerator and sets it beside her notebook. A car rumbles by outside, briefly sending a shaft of light across the curtained window. *I'll never get used to living so close to a road. I just want to go back home and have things the way they were.* But really, she knows things will never be back to how they were. At this point, though, she just wants to return to the canyon. She figures most of her nightmares probably come from that conversation she overheard her parents having. And the fact remains, they have *not* decided to go back or rebuild. *I'll die if I can't live in my beloved canyon.*

She opens the binder and stares at the empty page. It begs her to rectify the situation, somehow. *But how?* Pencil twiddling in her left hand, she thumps the eraser end on the wire spirals as flames come to mind—red hot, burning with a tint of blue, spewing forward into the mouth of the canyon she's called home her entire life. And then she sees a dragon and the words spill out onto the lines.

Images and story run onto the sheets of paper, exhausting her clenched fist trying to keep up. A peaceful village is destroyed in minutes by the wrath of a vengeful dragon whose motive stems from being awakened by the blasting in a neighboring mine. The once beautiful valley is left a burnt wasteland and the few survivors mill around the polluted river, wondering what to do.

An hour later, Brindle drops the pencil and shakes out her cramped fingers. Never before has she been able to write with this kind of fluidity. She enjoys writing, but she typically has to stop and think more between paragraphs. *Could writing stories be a way to ease my mind a little, even if it's related to what's eating me up these days?* She leans back in the chair and stretches, then rolls her head around to relieve the kink in her neck. *But there's got to be a way I can figure out how we can move back. The longer we're not there, the easier it will be for Mom and Dad not to return. But what?*

The guinea pig's movement enters her awareness again as she slumps down and closes her eyes. *I should just go to bed.* Following through with the notion, she shuts the notebook, sets her glass on the counter, turns out the light, and heads to the bedroom. *Maybe now I can get some sleep.*

Mom tells the class to put the *barres* away and stretch while she goes over her choreography notes. *It's kind of amazing how she can keep all the parts of* The Nutcracker *ballet organized in her head, and in that fat notebook. Sometimes it must get confusing.*

"Miss Val?" Randi asks. "How come we're changing the Chinese Dance this year?"

"That's a good question, Randi. There's been a lot of discussion about that lately, in the ballet world, concerning the integrity of that dance, in particular. You know how it's usually portrayed with uplifted index fingers?" She imitates the gesture and everyone nods. "And how the dancers' heads bob up and down with overly joyful faces?" She pauses. "Well, it can be viewed as insulting, embarrassing, and potentially racist."

Deanne rolls her eyes. "Really? Who would feel that way? I think it's cute." She slides into her right splits.

Annie looks at Mom and then Deanne. "You might feel differently if you were Chinese. Don't you think?"

"Oops," Deanne says. "You're half Chinese, aren't you?"

Annie nods. "But I never gave it much thought until Miss Val brought it up."

Brindle knows how hard Mom worked on revamping this dance and how she had to spend extra time in the studio to choreograph. Their family had discussed the ramifications of it, and now there will be a dragon from Chinatown, which is much more culturally specific and artful. "Who gets to be the dragon?"

Mom laughs and shakes her head. "That remains to be seen. Probably a few people since it's rather large. Maybe some parents. We'll see."

Brindle reaches forward from her wide straddle position on the floor and holds her forehead down. It's a nice stretch when you're fully warmed up. She thinks about the dragon in her story and wonders if any parallels can be drawn between hers and the one in *The Nutcracker.*

"Hey, Deanne? Sophia? Guess what."

"Huh?"

"I started writing a fantasy story. Would you like to read it and give me your feedback?"

This isn't the first time they've read each other's writing. The three musketeers love sharing books, movies, and their own stories, especially Brindle's.

"Sure," Deanne answers, rolling onto her stomach to push up and touch her feet to her head.

Sophia brings her straight legs together in front of her and shakes them out. "Yeah, just email it to me tonight."

Brindle agrees and everyone stands to practice *The Waltz of the Flowers.* She and Paige begin on stage left, while Sophia, Julie, and Annie start on the other side. They dance the beginning, the part they know thus far, and travel toward the center. The left side moves first, followed by the right. It's a very long piece with lots of *tour jetés* and they all know they'll have to pace themselves. The music is lovely and that helps to keep them dancing full out.

The framework of the ballet is beginning to take shape. This isn't the first time they've performed it, but these are new roles for Brindle and they're much more challenging. When class is finally over, Brindle is relieved. She hasn't been herself lately and she yawns. *Last night's writing must be catching up with me.* She unties her ribbons and eases the *pointe* shoes off her aching feet.

Randi slides over next to Paige. "Hey, my mom and I have been talking about that women's march in January. Do you still want to go?"

Brindle perks up when she hears this. They all had talked about it last spring and most of them wanted to go. Not Deanne, though.

Paige pulls a beanie over her dirty-blonde hair and answers. "Of course I do. And I think my mom still wants to, also."

"I think our whole family is going. Maybe we could all caravan." Brindle has never been to one of these women's marches, and she's very interested in anything that has to do with women's rights.

"Sounds like a plan," Randi says, before getting up to let the younger students come in. "See y'all." She waves at the remaining students gathered near the door and escorts her charges to the center of the studio.

Deanne leans over to Brindle. "Is your *whole* family really going to go? Even your dad?"

Brindle sighs, "Yes, Deanne, even my dad. He's always supported women's rights." She tries changing the subject. "Did you finish *Little Women* yet?"

Deanne pauses, digesting that last remark. "Almost—"

"I loved that book!" Paige exclaims. "Jo is such an inspiration, isn't she? Especially for her time."

"I think so, too," Brindle agrees.

"I liked it better than *Little Men*. I kind of had trouble getting into that one," Paige says.

Brindle continues talking to Paige, hoping Deanne will overhear. *Sometimes, it's easier to say something to someone else so when Deanne overhears, she has more time to absorb the information—without coming up with a response.* "It's nice to read books about strong women who don't kowtow to men, just because they're *expected* to."

"Mm hmm. But it must have been hard back then. Probably more difficult than it is now." Paige picks her things up off the floor.

"And more dangerous?"

"Absolutely," Paige adds. "We *have* to go to that women's march."

Brindle looks around and sees Deanne has wandered outside with Sophia. Sometimes she fantasizes about living in the past, but she knows she has more options now, as a female. She follows Paige outside as Deanne waves and gets in her car. Paige sits down on the sidewalk and opens her biology book.

"What are you studying in science these days?" Brindle knows Paige *loves* science and wants to be a scientist after college.

"Marie Curie." Paige looks up. "Have you heard of her?"

Brindle has. "Wasn't she a famous chemist?"

Paige turns slightly to avoid the glare from the parking lot. "Yeah, she sure was. She was the first woman to win two Nobel prizes. *And,* the first person to win them in two different scientific fields!"

"Wow." Brindle's interest piques and she sits down next to her. "What fields?"

Paige flips the pages and finds the spot. "It says here it was for physics and chemistry. And she was also the first female professor at the University of Paris." Her face flushes with joy.

Brindle leans over to look at the picture of the famous woman scientist. "She died early, at age sixty-six, from exposure to radiation!"

Paige runs her finger down the text. "Yeah, they didn't know about the dangers of radiation back in the early 1900s."

Brindle racks that up to another reason it might be better to live in these times, but she still wonders, sometimes, if she was born in the wrong century. She appreciates a lot of old-fashioned things more than many of the modern conveniences.

Paige gets up when she sees her mom's car and pauses for a moment. "I'm glad we talked, Brindle. It looks like we may have more in common than we knew." She turns away and waves, heading to the waiting sedan.

"Bye. See you Saturday!" Brindle smiles and realizes she's the only one left in front of the studio. *Paige is nice. And smart. It's not always easy to make friends, but somehow it feels easy with Paige.*

Finally, Dad pulls up and Willow jumps out of the car and runs past her into the studio.

Why is she always in such a hurry? Brindle gathers her things so she and Dad can go home and figure out dinner.

10

A MINI TRIP

Paige

Keep your spot strong while traveling across the diagonal.

Paige's mouth waters as she peels the banana she'd packed for her after-rehearsal snack. She'd been daydreaming about a ham and cheese sandwich on whole wheat bread, but this is her new reality. She wishes she had almond butter to go with it. *That stuff is a good addition to apples or bananas.*

"I like to eat, eat, eat apples and bananas," she sings quietly, bopping her head as she walks to the trash can to deposit the peel.

Randi joins in on the second verse. "I like to ate, ate, ate ay-ples and ba-nay-nays."

The girls giggle and continue the song and Miss Val looks up.

"Maybe we should put on a musical instead of a ballet? You girls sound pretty good." She covers the stereo with a pink cloth, to keep off the ever-present Nuevo dust, and carries her choreography notebook to the desk. "The PVC pipes for Drosselmeyer's gift frame are in that bag by the door. Paige, are you still interested in putting it together?"

"Yup, I certainly am." She smiles and *chassés* over to begin the project.

Miss Val pauses. "It's good to have you back, Paige. I mean, you seem to be back to your old chipper self."

Paige beams. "I am. I'm feeling *so* much better now. I kind of miss all those yummy things like donuts and *normal* sandwiches. But as long as I'm diligent about what I eat, I'm good."

Randi steals a cashew out of Paige's baggie. "You've lost weight, too, haven't you? You look great!" She gives her friend a good-hearted slap on the back.

"Ow!" Paige mocks. "But thanks. And yes, I have lost weight. Five pounds, to be exact."

Deanne comes back in with Jack and Todd, directing them where to set the massive arch they're carrying.

"Careful of the light!" Annie yells.

Sophia covers her mouth at the near miss. "Good save!"

"That was close," Brindle says.

After the boys, with Deanne's assistance, set down the large prop, they step back to analyze it.

"I think the base needs to be a little wider so it won't fall down as easily. What do you think?" Miss Val asks.

"Do you have any longer boards in the truck?" asks Jack.

"Yes," Miss Val says and Brindle goes out to get them.

Deanne walks around the future throne, where Clara and the Nutcracker prince will sit. "It's kind of plain. And ugly."

"Hey, wait a minute here. I personally take offense to that, Deanne," Todd states dramatically. "I think it's rather beautiful, myself," he adds, but can't help laughing.

"All it needs is a coat of paint and some sparkles, and then, *voilà*, it's a piece of art!" Jack laughs along with the rest of them and takes the boards from Brindle when she returns.

Todd drapes his arm around Randi's shoulders. This has become a more regular occurrence lately and Paige can't help feeling a little left out.

Paige seizes the moment to fetch her water out of her ballet bag and takes a long drink. *If only this was horchata.*

The crew spends the next hour working on props for their show and clowning around with each other. Paige is looking forward to 3 p.m. when her dad is actually coming to pick her up and take her to LA to spend the weekend with him.

It's about time. I haven't seen him in months. He's been too busy, evidently, to spend time with me. Her parents have been divorced for years and they've maintained a decent relationship. But lately she's been feeling a little abandoned by her dad.

Sure enough, right on time, he pulls up to get her. She bids her comrades farewell and approaches the unfamiliar black sports car as he rolls down the window.

"A new Corvette?" She quickly thinks about how many hours Mom works just to drive a regular car and put food on their table.

"Yup. Ya like her?" He smiles his big winning smile.

I thought that grin was mostly to impress the ladies.

His smile warms and Paige says, "Hi, Dad."

"How are you, darling? I've missed you." He pushes a button and unlocks her door.

She starts to put her bags behind the seat, but there's no space. He gets out and takes them from her and tosses them into the trunk. After a quick hug Paige slides into the soft, white leather. Once they're both safely buckled in, Dad backs out of the parking space, smoothly navigates the lot, and zooms into traffic.

"May the journey begin!" He smiles at her again and she starts to relax.

"So, Dad, what are we going to do this weekend?" Paige stares at the pristine dashboard, and wonders what on earth all those knobs and gauges are for.

"Well—" he begins. "I've got a new condo and I thought you might like to hang out there for a bit."

"You moved?"

"Yeah. The other place was kind of cramped, you know?" He accelerates to overtake a slow-moving propane truck. "I think you'll like it."

"Okay, I guess so," she responds, not sure of what else to say.

They spend the remainder of the ride with mostly polite pleasantries—nothing of real substance. And eventually, Paige closes her eyes and dozes off.

◆

She wakes to the click of the car doors unlocking. "Are we there?"

Dad laughs. "Yes, we are." He laughs again. "You were zonked, kiddo. I even picked up dinner on the way!"

"Really? I slept through *that*?" She rubs her eyes, disbelievingly. "I *have* been more tired lately."

"Okay, well, time to grab your things and come on in." Dad opens the trunk of the car and lifts out the bags.

The condo complex looks more like row houses, or something she pictures might be in San Francisco. Each one is a different color, and actually, quite pleasing to the eye.

"This looks nice, Dad." She approaches the front steps and he opens the carved front door for her.

"*Entre vous*," he says, bowing slightly to her as she enters.

"*Merci*," she responds in kind, wondering about the sudden change in language. *Maybe he's a little nervous, too.*

The living room floor looks like expensive hardwood, and there's a large area rug in the middle. It's sparsely but elegantly furnished with a sectional sofa; a big-screen, wall-mounted television; and lawyer-style bookcases. *Dad is an attorney, after all.* He tells her that the spiral staircase leads to a loft and bedroom upstairs.

"The kitchen's that-a-way." Dad points toward a corner of the room. "And the guest room is through here."

Paige follows him past "the guest bathroom" into the small bedroom where she will sleep tonight. She drops her heavy totes onto the grey bedspread and walks over to the window.

"Pretty, huh?"

"Yeah," she says. A well-manicured lawn and flowers are lit by one of those lamps that point upward to illuminate trees. "I can't believe it's dark already."

"Well, it's not summer anymore." He sets down her other bag on a chair next to the door. "You hungry?"

"I'm starved. What's for dinner?" *I'm hoping it's not what I think it is, but the smell makes me suspect it is.*

"I picked up a pepperoni pizza while you were sleeping. As I recall, it's your favorite."

Paige's salivary glands start to come alive with anticipation. "But I can't eat that anymore, remember? Mom and I told you."

"I know. But it's just once. For old time's sake." He wraps her in a hug. "Paige, I've missed you so much."

"I've missed you, too, Dad." She looks up into his eyes, reassured. "But, really, I'm not supposed to eat anything with gluten or dairy in it. And pizza has both."

"Oh, you'll be fine. Trust me." Dad lets go of her and turns to leave. "Let's hurry up and have dinner before it gets cold. At 7:00 I've got a Zoom meeting that will take the rest of the evening." He peers over his wire-framed glasses. "Come on." He motions for her to follow and walks out of the room.

I really want to believe him. Pepperoni pizza is my absolute favorite. And I do miss it so much. Maybe just this once. Besides, he probably doesn't have anything else I can eat here anyway.

She follows him into the kitchen and sees the large pizza box sitting on the counter. When he opens the lid, the most magnificent aroma fills the room. She pulls up the first slice and strands of mozzarella pull away from the rest of the thick, gooey masterpiece. She places it onto a plate and then takes the can of soda Dad offers her.

"I haven't had one of these in ages, either."

Once seated at the dining room table, they clink cans. She sinks her teeth into the greasy cheese and pepperoni sensation. Her eyes close and she wraps her attention around this amazing culinary experience. *Pizza has never tasted this good before.*

"My meeting starts in fifteen minutes. The remote for the TV is on the end cabinet, next to the sofa in the living room." He gets up to grab another piece of pizza and asks if she'd like one, too.

Paige nods and washes her bite down with a gulp of soda. "How long have you lived in this place, Dad?"

"Oh, not long. Maybe a couple months. I hired a gal at work to help me decorate. Do you like it?"

Paige scans the minimalist, modern-looking space and shrugs. "It's nice." She nods. *But it's certainly not very homey—or inviting.*

Dad takes their plates into the open kitchen and deposits them in the dishwasher.

"Well, good night, Paige." He smiles his big grin and comes over to give her a kiss on the top of her head. "See you in the morning." He starts to leave, but turns back. "Maybe we could go out to breakfast in the morning?"

"Sure, Dad. Good night." She picks up her napkin and wipes her mouth, watching him make his exit.

Twenty minutes later, she runs to the small bathroom and explodes from both ends. Her innards roil with excruciating waves of nausea and cramping, forcing every bit of that pizza and soda out.

Why did I eat that? With this thought, it begins all over again.

Images of rapid gunfire amid hilly terrain careen through her brain. The bullets ricochet and sear into the beautiful landscape, leaving gaping holes in the aftermath. *Is this what leaky gut syndrome looks like?*

She closes her eyes and sinks down to the floor, hugging the toilet. But then she's forced back up onto it as more violent waves roar within. The next two hours are not pleasant, that's for sure. *I will never eat pizza again!*

The battle scene in *The Nutcracker* comes to mind with the rats fighting the soldiers. Swords a flyin', rats a spookin'... She manages a laugh in spite of her situation. *It feels like those soldiers are poking swords into my stomach and then twisting them, for good measure. Leaky gut syndrome?*

She wants to tell Dad, but he'd said he was going to be busy the rest of the evening and had already said good night. She thinks about calling Mom, but decides against it. *She works so hard and almost never gets any time alone. Besides, after dealing with everyone else's problems all day, she hardly needs to listen to mine right now. There's nothing she can do about it anyway.*

Paige peels herself away from the bathroom and heads weakly into the living room. She finds the remote, clicks on the TV, and flops down on the couch. As she flips channels, her body slowly reclines to the side and she leans into a big, soft pillow.

Ads, ads, and more ads. Finally, there's a show about dance. *At least there are teenagers dancing on a stage in glitzy costumes.* They shimmy and shake and then end in a striking pose, and the televised audience claps and shouts. An announcer thanks the group for "coming all this way" and announces the next contestant.

"Now we have Kate James from Chicago, doing a hip-hop piece!"

The tiny dancer bops, turns, and ignites the stage and the judges hold up their grades. Next, the cameras move backstage to interview the next contestant and her mother—mostly her mother. The young scrawny girl can't seem to get a word in between the large woman's bragging.

"Yes, she's worked very hard, and we've hired the absolute best coaches. I really believe she's going to win." Then she leans into the microphone and says in a softer voice, "She'll at least beat the one who's in first place right now."

A scuffle follows when another mom crowds in and gives her a shove.

Paige shakes her head, annoyed at these women's poor behavior. "Grow up," she says out loud. Giving in to her lethargy, she sinks farther down into the sofa.

"And now we have Dina from Tallahassee!"

This dark-haired, exotic beauty radiates confidence, if not snobbishness, and glides through an acrobatic ballet dance.

She is really good. But the sentiment vanishes once the young *lady* opens her mouth during the brief interview afterward. She badmouths the other contestants, just like that mother did, and Paige can't stand it anymore. *Too much pressure for the girls and a battle zone for their mothers.*

The next morning, Dad agrees to drive Paige back early since she's still not feeling well. They have to pull over once for her to dry-heave into the weeds. *Probably because I was too scared to eat anything for breakfast and I'm so hungry my stomach hurts.* When they arrive, he walks her into the house and sets her bags on the couch. Mom appears and confronts him. They had already talked on the phone.

"How could you give her pizza? You knew about her gluten intolerance. We told you weeks ago!"

"You didn't get that diagnosis from a real doctor. How do you know what's really going on?" He's backing toward the door now.

Mom huffs with exasperation. "Just go, okay?"

"All right," Dad says. "Well, Paige—I'm glad you're feeling better. It's probably just a touch of the flu or something. See you next month."

All she can do is sort of wave from the recliner that has now claimed her body. Mom closes the door behind him.

"Sometimes that man makes my blood boil!" Mom walks over and strokes her hair. "Do you need anything, honey?"

"Maybe some juice? And I'll just reacquaint myself with this comfy chair for the day—if you don't mind."

"Paige?" Mom pauses. "Perhaps you won't be tempted next time? This new eating program seems to be helping, don't you think?"

"Yeah. I won't ever make *that* mistake again." And then she drifts off into dreamland, albeit back to *The Nutcracker* battle scene, and the images of leaky gut syndrome.

11

Día de los Muertos

Brindle

*To know oneself well, we must
put ourselves out there.*

The three musketeers gather around a large book at a back table in the local library, where they like to go between dance classes. Being well read, Brindle has heard about *El Día de los Muertos* and continues to be curious about it—especially now that Halloween is almost here.

"I think it's so cool that your family celebrates this holiday, Sophia."

"Yeah—oh, hey, I read your dragon story. It was great! Did you read it yet, Deanne?"

"Mm hmm. It's awesome. Was it an assignment from school?"

"No, I just felt like writing it."

Deanne stares at Brindle. "You wrote that whole thing just for fun? It wasn't even an assignment?"

"Maybe you could turn it in for extra credit or something," Sophia suggests.

"Ha. I don't believe you guys. Don't you ever write anything just for fun?"

Deanne and Sophia make a face and Deanne says, "Not something *that* long."

The three of them laugh good-naturedly.

Brindle adds, "I like to write. Besides, having to turn it in for a grade might take the joy out of it."

Deanne leans over her two friends sitting in front of her. "These are amazing pictures. Are they dressed up for Halloween?"

"No, Deanne. I think those are from *All Souls' Day* or *The Day of the Dead*." Sophia turns the page and Deanne walks around to sit on the opposite side of the table.

"Didn't the celebration actually start with the Aztecs? I think I read that somewhere." Brindle starts scanning the text.

"My father says it's some pagan holiday. I like it, but it sometimes gives me the creeps." She stares at the photographs in the book, then adds, "I just don't like thinking about dead people. It makes me feel like throwing up."

Brindle and Sophia both lift their focus to her.

Sophia starts to laugh, but stops. She looks down at the page before continuing. "We believe that death is a natural part of our lifecycle and try to think of it not as a day of sadness, but a day of celebration. It feels like they wake up and sort of celebrate with us."

"Does your family build an altar for them?" Brindle asks.

"Sometimes. And sometimes we leave out their favorite food, too."

Deanne crinkles her nose. "Doesn't it smell after a while?"

Sophia laughs. "Well, we don't leave it out forever."

Brindle looks at all the bright colors. "And marigolds, too. What's with all the flowers anyway?" She runs her finger down the lines. "Oh, it says here that their bright colors help to guide the spirits to the altars, plus their pungent scent." Brindle stops and holds up a finger. "Just a sec." She quickly walks to the main desk and checks out a laptop. When she returns, both girls look up.

"What are you up to now?" Deanne asks.

"I need to start doing some major research."

"For school?" Sophia asks, leaning over to peer at the computer screen.

Brindle waits for the device to turn on. It's all too painful to think about, but unless she can figure out a way to get her family back into the canyon, the hurt will grow even more. *Unbearable.* "Well," she begins. "My parents aren't sure they want to rebuild our house."

"What?" both girls ask in unison.

"What if they sell our land and buy something else?" Brindle's eyes begin to sting, but she wills back the tears. "You guys know that would kill me, right?"

"You love that place so much," Deanne says.

"It's the only home you've ever known, isn't it?" Sophia puts a hand on Brindle's shoulder.

"That's why I have to figure out how to get us back home soon—before they get used to living somewhere else." Brindle starts googling things: rebuilding after a fire, alternative construction, the tiny house movement....

Sophia and Deanne sit on each side of Brindle, taking turns pointing at the screen and commenting on what they see. Brindle speed-reads through pages of information, gathering data in her mind.

"Look here," Brindle says. "Lots of people, these days, are choosing minimalism as a lifestyle."

"What does that even mean?" Sophia asks.

Brindle reads further. "They decide they don't need as much stuff as regular households have, you know, like dishwashers, walk-in closets with more clothes than one could possibly wear, extra kitchen gadgets—"

"I don't think I'd like that," Deanne says. "Look how small that place is."

Brindle studies the compact kitchenette with a small single sink and pull-out table. "It's a tiny house and it looks like there's a ton of hidden storage built into it."

"My big family sure wouldn't fit into that," Sophia says. "Not with all my little brothers, anyway. Maybe I could just live there by myself; then I'd have enough room."

The girls laugh and Deanne says, "Yeah, like that would ever happen." They laugh again.

Brindle clicks through more sites. "Well, we don't have much stuff anymore. It all burned up. So maybe—" She pauses in thought. "Maybe my family could live in something really small while we build something bigger." Again, she's lost in thought. *This is going to take more time.*

Deanne glances down at her phone. "Hey, we better go. Your mom's probably already here."

The girls gather their things and Brindle goes to return the laptop and check out the *Día de los Muertos* book. She has an insatiable curiosity. Glancing over the various flyers laying on the counter, she picks one advertising an event at the art gallery.

"Hey, check this out," she says, handing the paper to Deanne.

Deanne takes it from her and Sophia looks on.

"We should *so* go to this, don't you think?" Deanne asks.

"Yeah," Brindle says, putting the book into her backpack.

Sophia continues to study it. "Hey, it's this Friday night! I'll ask my mom when we get in the car."

On the short ride back over to the studio, Sophia's little brothers argue relentlessly in the back two seats of the van.

Sophia's mom barks at them. "*Silencio, por favor!*"

"Hey, Mom?" Sophia begins. "There's an opening at the art gallery on Friday night and it's about *El Día de los Muertos!* Can we go?"

"What, us, our family? Or you three musketeers?" She laughs.

"Us three," Sophia answers.

"That sounds like fun. Did you girls know that the altars are called *ofrendas,* and that on that day, we pray for and remember our friends and family members who have passed on? We believe we can help support their spiritual journey."

Brindle takes it all in. "Fascinating." *I'd like to believe that, too. It must be nice to have that kind of connection with so many generations—past and present.* She looks over at Deanne, who's staring out the window. *I'm surprised she wants to go since this isn't really her thing. But, at least she's game—and I like that about her.*

They pull into the parking lot and pile out of the van, discussing the details of their Friday night adventure. When Brindle opens the studio door, a rush of warm, humid air greets her. *Nothing like exercise to heat up a room.* The Intermediate ballet class has just ended and Mom is taking tuition payments from a couple people at the desk. The girls quickly strip down to their dance attire and hurry onto the floor. It's time for the Contemporary dance class to begin.

"Let's start with some nice, slow, relaxing head rolls while I cue up the music, okay?"

Several other dancers have joined them, including a couple of women who only take this class, not ballet, too.

Mom glides to the front and leads the group in an impromptu, changing the leader, kind of warmup. She doesn't do this often, and Brindle's not all that fond of it. She prefers more structure and not being put on the spot. *Deanne seems to like it, though, and Mom says it's good for us—it helps with our improv skills. Another thing I don't really care for.*

When Brindle leads the class, she repeats an old pattern she remembers from last year. Then Deanne takes charge with Martha Graham contractions on the floor and a fun swing series she'd obviously learned somewhere else. She has them start in a wide *seconde* position, in turnout—reach to the right side, release downward with the breath, pause to the left, and return. Then repeat forward and back and in different positions. By the end of her exercise, everyone is breathing hard.

"Okay, quick stretch, everyone, and then we'll do our October pattern for the last time!"

Brindle really likes this pattern. It's often bittersweet to dance something for the last time, especially when the music for this one is such a fantastic violin solo. She's even been listening to it while she does her schoolwork. It's *that* good!

Brindle positions herself to the right of Deanne and slightly in front of Sophia. The piece begins in a statuesque pose, which reminds her of a Greek sculpture representing a young maiden holding some sort of tray over her head. Her legs are crossed and the other arm is wrapped around her own waist. Looking upward with a slight smile, the notes begin. She slowly twists and untwists at first, followed by Martha Graham-type pleading movements on the ground. Off-balance turns, layouts, acrobatic leaps, and contortions in the choreography allow her to inhabit another realm. *Kind of like an actor does?*

"Good work, everyone!" Miss Val applauds them at the finish. "I have to say, I'll be sad to see this dance go. Maybe I'll have to hang onto my notes for this one."

Often, during the last fifteen minutes of the last class of the month, they are encouraged to work on their own choreography. But it's not just for fun. Mom gives them pointers about what is working and what may need a little help.

"Hey, Brindle!" Deanne comes over with Sophia. "Let's work together, okay?"

"Sure," Brindle responds, as Mom begins to play the music they'll be choreographing to. It's a complicated percussion piece with very little melody. As usual, Deanne takes the lead.

"I've got an idea. Sophia, you start by lying down in front here." Deanne points to the floor. "And, Brindle, pick a mid-height pose, okay? And you can be there. I'll do some kind of reaching thing back here."

They come up with a starting pose and then, as a group, decide to do a boogie-woogie type freestyle for the next sixteen counts, moving around in a haphazard way—bumping into each other the second time they practice it. Sophia laughs hysterically and Deanne giggles. Brindle gives a half-hearted laugh and then yawns. *I'm hungry and I just want to go home.* But *home* is *not* where they live now and it continues to bother her. Again. It's all she can do to just go through the motions and get through to the end of class. She wonders if she will ever find a way to return home— for good. *How, and what will it take?*

After dinner, Brindle goes outside to hang with their dog. She scratches behind his ears and he follows her out to the swing in the backyard. The moon is a narrow sliver, slowly sliding down in its descent toward the western horizon.

"Oh, Nutkins, what are we going to do?" She pats the top of his soft head, and eases onto the wooden plank. Her loyal friend sits beside her, dutifully, as she gently pushes her weight back and forth, her feet never leaving the ground. The night air is warm and inviting and she closes her eyes, leaning her head against the side-chain. Her companion grunts quietly and then lies down with a flop.

A few minutes later, she hears the back door close and Mom comes out and parks herself in the chair next to the swing set. Nutkins pads over to get another dose of attention.

"It sure is a beautiful night, isn't it?" Mom sips her usual mug of herbal tea.

"Mm hmm." Brindle closes her eyes again. "Hey, Mom?"

"Yes?"

"I want to go home."

"I know."

"I do. I mean, I really do. This isn't *bad,* but it's *not* home. Can we go back tomorrow? Just for a little while?" She opens her eyes and turns to face her.

"I promised Willow and Taz we would get their costumes tomorrow. Thursday is Halloween." Mom wraps both hands around her cup. "And Friday you guys want to go to that art exhibit, right?"

Brindle weighs her options. "Uh huh." *Well, at least there's that. I can sort of look forward to that, I guess.*

On Friday evening, Brindle's family drives over to pick up Deanne to go see the *Día de los Muertos* display at the art gallery. Sophia's family is going, too, so the girls will meet up there.

Brindle leans over when Deanne gets in the car and whispers, "I didn't know if you would get to come or not."

"Hmm? Why not?" Deanne asks, fastening her seatbelt.

"Well—it's not exactly the sort of thing your family appreciates, is it?"

Deanne laughs mischievously. "I only said we were going to an art exhibit."

"Oh, I see." Brindle snickers, too.

They arrive to a very crowded gathering. People move in and out of the building bearing drinks and snacks, chattering away like they haven't seen each other in years.

"This is quite an event," Mom says as she closes the car door behind her.

Dad puts his arm around her and ushers her inside, with Willow following closely behind.

"Hey, Brindle?"

"Yeah, Taz?"

"Will there be dead people in there?"

Brindle places a hand on her little brother's head. "No. I think it's more about offerings and artwork to honor those who aren't here anymore."

Taz pulls up short. "How will dead people know this is for them?"

Good question. "I'm not sure. Why don't you go ask Mom or Dad?"

He thinks for a moment and then dashes ahead to catch up with them.

"Look, there's Sophia!" Deanne points and their friend *chassés* toward them.

The three musketeers giggle their way inside and stop to survey the refreshment table. A fanned array of exotic cheeses lies within a wreath of green, red, and purple grapes. An assortment of crackers and chips nestle into handmade baskets, and wine and sparkling water are available on the antique buffet. On yet another surface, Halloween candy abounds.

"It's like early trick-or-treating," Brindle says.

"*La extraño eso*," Sophia muses.

"What's that mean?" Brindle asks.

"It means I miss it. You know, going trick-or-treating."

"Me, too," Brindle agrees.

"Well, I was never *allowed* to go, remember?"

The girls affirm, as everyone knows Deanne's Dad's stance on Halloween. But, this year, Brindle and Sophia had decided they were probably getting a little old to go out and beg for candy. Besides, they don't want to rub Deanne's nose in something she isn't part of.

A one-eyed ghost walks by, arm-in-arm with a scary-looking ghoul.

Deanne stares. "I didn't know people got dressed up for this Day of the Dead thing."

"I think those are Halloween costumes, don't you?"

Brindle says, "Yeah, probably."

There are so many little homemade altars everywhere: sitting on shelves, tacked to walls, hanging from bars....

A lot of them have crucifixes. There are papier mâché dolls depicting departed loved ones, skulls on sticks, and marigolds everywhere—oranges, reds, and yellows.

The place is alive with color and Brindle can feel the vibrations pulsing around the event. Lively music comes from somewhere near the back and the wall-to-wall people make it hard to see everything. Before long, she's had enough and excuses herself to go outside. *Crowds can be a little hard to take sometimes.* She finds a bench in the little garden area outside, but has to put up with some guy smoking nearby. Eventually, Deanne comes to find her.

"I think your parents are ready to go. Are you?"

"Yeah. You know how much I *love* crowds."

They head to the car and arrive at the same time as the rest of her family.

"Wasn't that terrific?" Dad asks.

He's super energized by the evening. As a history professor, he's interested in all these kinds of things. *Perhaps that's where I get it from. It's too bad the show isn't going to stay up longer because it would be nice to actually be able to check out everything here, without all the people. Oh well.*

After class and rehearsal on Saturday, the Advanced ballet students assemble at Brindle's house to paint the throne and chairs for *The Nutcracker.* Jack, Todd, Randi, and Paige carry the large arch from the bed of Mom's white truck to the back patio. Brindle, Sophia, and Deanne hurry to finish covering the slab with tarps before the heavy prop gets there.

"Hold on!" Deanne yells. "Almost done. There! Go ahead."

Annie and Julie smooth out the wrinkles in the plastic as the monster prop is set down.

"Good job, guys!" Mom appears from the house and points to the paints and supplies they can use. "I've got a pot of beans on the stove and a fresh loaf of bread from the Farmer's Market. And for you, my dear—" She drapes her arm over Paige's shoulders. "We also have a small round of gluten-free sourdough."

Paige claps her hands. "Oh, thank you, Miss Val. You remembered!"

"Of course."

Mom disappears back inside as the dancers get to work. Brindle picks up a medium-sized brush while Jack opens the white paint. Deanne grabs a long-bristled wide one and dips it into the liquid, then drips all the way over to the side she's decided to start on.

"Whoa, Deanne!" Annie laughs. "We got those tarps down in the nick of time, didn't we?"

Deanne teases back, "Didn't you have a modeling job to go to or something?"

"Not today, I didn't. But I have one at the college tomorrow."

"I heard college is a lot more fun than high school. Is it?" Sophia asks.

"Definitely."

Todd and Randi carry over the two chairs and start coating them with metallic silver.

"How pretty!" Sophia says. "Can I help paint those?"

"Get a brush," Todd says and stands shoulder-to-shoulder to Randi, putting his hand over hers as she strokes the back of the chair.

"Get your own brush," she teases, pressing her weight into him, causing him to stumble off balance and almost land in the five-gallon bucket of rinse water.

He over-exaggerates the move and then says, with hands on his hips and chin up high, "Huh! Well, I don't want to share with you, either." He stomps his foot dramatically and strides over to get his own tool of the trade. "Mine's better, anyway."

"Such drama," Annie says, rolling her eyes, and everyone cracks up at the ongoing antics, something Todd always provides in abundance. "We love you anyway, Todd."

He smiles back at the group and wiggles in exaggerated satisfaction.

What a clown. Brindle gets a warm fuzzy feeling inside. Every so often, it strikes her how lucky she is to be part of this *dance family.* They really do care for one another. Without them, and Sophia and Deanne, she may not have *any* friends. She's certainly not a social butterfly. *But these are my people.* She smiles and turns back to the painting job at hand.

12

ALL TOGETHER NOW

Paige

Be supportive of your fellow dancers.

Randi and Todd walk in through the open studio door, hand in hand. Paige glances over at them and smiles politely.

I miss the way we used to be together. It's sad that things have to change, but I do sort of understand. Paige lifts the lid of her shoebox and pulls the tissue aside, revealing the brand-new *pointe* shoes. She had just sewn the ribbons and elastics on the night before.

"Oh, whoa, whoa, whoa, Paige! Let me see them!" Randi calls, hurrying over, leaving Todd behind. She grabs the box, buries her nose into the crinkly paper, and takes a deep whiff, closing her eyes.

Paige laughs. "More like smell them, you mean." *That girl definitely has a thing for the scent of new toe shoes.*

Deanne giggles, too. "You're so weird, Randi."

"What? Don't you guys like the smell?"

"Well, yeah. But—" Paige teases. "We're just not so hound-doggish about it."

"That's funny. Good one, Paige," Todd says and puts his arm around Randi's shoulders. "She's just a little *special* is all."

The group surrounding them cracks up and Randi meows at him sarcastically and pretends to scratch him.

"See what I mean?" he says, snickering with the rest of them.

Paige takes the box from Randi and begins the process of cramming her feet into the shoes and tying the ribbons just so—crossing them in front of her ankles, then behind, followed by wrapping them around to tie on the outside.

"Don't forget to tuck in the ends," Randi teases. "We wouldn't want you to trip on them, would we?"

"Okay, point taken." Paige grins at her old friend, grateful they can still joke around with each other. She stands up and leans into her right foot, forcing the arch and full *pointe* of her toes. The new shoes have that beautiful pink sheen that, unfortunately, won't last long.

"They're so pretty," Julie, the new girl, says. "How long have you had toe shoes?"

"This is my second year. I kind of got a late start," Paige answers, now leaning into her other foot. "I don't think I worked the arch enough before I put them on."

"What do you mean? Don't they come ready? I mean, they're brand new, aren't they?" She stares at the hard shoes.

"Hey, Randi, can you show Julie your old shoes? Let her feel how broken-in they get?"

"Sure. I think I have a really old pair in my bag." Randi bends over, her legs fully straightened, which stretches the hamstrings, and digs around in her large purple bag with the images of leaping kitty cats. "Here's one of them." She holds up a limp, dirty, scuffed-up, sorry excuse for a once-beautiful specimen.

"Wow," Julie says, crinkling her nose and grasping the frayed, pinkish ribbon from which the shoe is dangling. She takes the heel in one hand and the toe in another and bends it back and forth. "I didn't know they could get this soft. They're almost like regular ballet slippers."

"Well," Paige says. "They certainly never *feel* like them. At least not to me, they don't."

Randi laughs. "This is true." She takes the old shoe and tosses it back into her bag when Miss Val walks out to start their *barre* exercises.

"Okay, you all know how we do this," Miss Val says. "Today is our first full rehearsal, so we have a lot to accomplish and we need to stay focused. We'll do a short *barre* and then rehearse the dances. Then in about an hour-and-a-half, the Beginners and Intermediates will join us to practice the whole ballet, almost."

"What about all the other kids, like the gymnasts and tappers?" Sophia asks, from her place behind Deanne.

Miss Val smiles and shakes her head. "You really ought to read the handouts I give you." She turns to face the *barre,* places both elbows on it, and rests her head in her hands.

She looks tired. It must be exhausting to go through what their family did. "They don't come for a couple weeks, right?"

"Thank you, Paige. Anyway, yes, we have four full rehearsals here in the studio and the gymnasts come to the last two. Both the gymnasts and tappers will have their own rehearsals and they'll join us at the dress rehearsal on stage." She looks over at Sophia again, raising her eyebrows, and then smiles.

"Okaaay. I get it now."

Brindle pats her friend's head good-naturedly as Miss Val continues.

"So, when the others arrive, you can have a short break while they warm up and run through their dances. Except you, right, Randi?"

"Right, Miss Val." Randi straightens up and gets into first position.

Paige would like to hang out with her friend during the break, but she knows Randi has to help out with the younger dancers. She moves through the *pliés, tendus, dégagés, ronde de jambs, frappés,* and *grand battements* with surprising energy. *I'm so excited we're finally in full rehearsals! This is when the whole ballet starts to take shape.*

After a very brief stretch, the dancers rise and get into their positions to begin Act One, the Christmas Eve party at Dr. and Mrs. Stahlbaum's. Randi and Jack stand together in center stage as Clara (Deanne) points at the invisible decorations on the currently nonexistent tree and pretends to interact with Fritz (who will join them later, when the younger classes arrive).

After walking through Act One with no music, while Miss Val counts the phrasing and coaches along the way, the music finally begins. Although it's not a dress rehearsal, Paige has brought her ballerina doll costume so she can practice making the quick change during Act One. As soon as she's on stage, as a party guest, she exits behind the stool that serves as the tree for now. She quickly pulls on the sequined pink leotard with the tutu attached. It fits a little better now that she's lost a few pounds, but she barely gets it on in enough time to creep behind Drosselmeyer's big present, which at this point is still invisible. The old one burned up with most of the other props and they haven't finished creating a new one yet.

After Mike drags her out, she does three sudden jerks to stand up. *Oh no, my pointe shoe is untied! Too late now.* At the end of her short solo she trips, but then scoots backward off stage right to change again, retie her shoe, and come back on in her original attire. *Will I make it on time?*

It takes Paige longer and Miss Val stops the music to wait for her to hurry into place for the March Dance. The scene ends with the group walking across the front of the stage (studio) as if going home after the party, dragging their sleepy children through the streets of London.

Todd strides over to Deanne and bows in a ridiculous spoofing manner when it's time to run through their Clara and Nutcracker duet—after skipping the battle scene.

He obviously likes this part. And it looks like Deanne is beginning to lighten up a little and enjoy it, too. He's such a goof-off, but he is funny.

When the piece begins, he helps her up and they stand next to each another with one arm behind the other's back and the opposite stretched forward, holding hands. Her hand, of course, is on top. It's just the way it's done.

Halfway through the piece, when they're standing side-by-side in upstage (back) center, Miss Val stops the music.

"Let's go over this again, from here." She dances in front of Todd so he can mimic her movements as Deanne mirrors them. "One, two, three, four." Miss Val slowly does a *temps lié* forward, transferring her weight from one leg to the other while changing arms. Todd copies the movements behind and then they repeat, shifting backward.

How can Miss Val be so focused when their whole family lost everything only a couple months ago?

When Deanne and Todd try it again with music, Paige notices how much better it is.

It is kind of romantic when they parade around in such a regal fashion. This feigned chivalry is a little ridiculous. But, who knows? Maybe this practice of etiquette, especially for the boys, might lead to less burping and shoving.

Paige hobbles over to the left back corner when Miss Val announces *The Waltz of the Flowers*. Her feet are killing her and she asks Miss Val if it would be all right to take her *pointe* shoes off and wear ballet slippers.

"Okay, hurry up then," Miss Val says, and reminds Sophia, Annie, and Julie, who are on stage right, to make sure to wait sixteen counts after the intro to enter.

Paige leaps over from stage right, where her ballet tote is, back to her starting place, after briefly brushing her feet in the rosin box. Her slippers haven't been worn much lately and she wants to make sure she doesn't slip.

She and Brindle wait out the intro before traveling toward center stage with a *sauté, tombé, glissade, assemblé battu.* Then they dance slightly downstage left executing a *cabriole, tombé, glissade, pas de chat.* While the other two make their entrance using the same movements, but in reverse, they wait in fifth position—with Paige slightly downstage right of Brindle.

Later, in the *waltz turn* circle, Paige gets dizzy and veers off course. Once on the straightaway, with a simple traveling pattern, she shakes her head. *I think I need to eat something.* With this new diet of junk-free eating, she has to graze more often or she gets light-headed. Luckily, as soon as the dance is over, Miss Val calls their break and Paige walks over to retrieve a granola bar before heading outside with the others. The younger students crowd in as soon as the door opens.

"What do you have?" Brindle asks, biting into a small green apple.

"Just this." Paige holds up her snack.

Brindle nods and Sophia rips open her bag of Cheetos, joining them.

"Those look delicious." Paige's mouth waters. "And aren't they gluten-free?"

"I think so, but this is healthier," Brindle assures her with a smile. She takes a huge bite. "Mmm! This is *so* good!" She continues to exaggerate the deliciousness of her apple, going on and on about it.

"No one's buying it, Brindle," Sophia says, chuckling.

This strikes Brindle as funny and her grin grows into a sputtering fit of laughter. She then runs over to the weeds next to the building to spit out the green fragments, before she chokes on them. She continues giggling. "Oh, you don't know what you're missing!"

"Uh, I'm pretty sure we do." Todd looks sideways at her and then back at the group before starting his own little comedy act.

Oh no. What's he going to do?

Todd grabs Paige's granola bar and tears into it. "Oh! My, my, my, my!" He takes a gigantic bite. And then he crams the rest of it into his mouth and starts moaning. "Mmm. Oh. Mmm mm mmm!" He obviously *can't* say anything else with his mouth so full, so he starts rubbing his belly and repeats, "Mm mmm!" He licks around his lips in a grand gesture. "Mmm hmm!"

Deanne is cracking up now and the rest of them can't help it, either.

Even Paige laughs. *But I was really looking forward to eating that.* "Todd! That's the only thing I brought to eat today! You owe me a granola bar!" *What am I going to have now?*

As if reading her mind, Brindle opens a bag of almonds and offers her some.

"Thanks." She puts her arm around her while glaring at Todd. "You're the best, Brindle."

"I'm sorry," Todd admits. "But I was so *awfully* hungry." He starts rubbing his stomach again, appreciatively, and they all laugh again. "No hard feelings?" he asks with his pleading puppy-dog look.

"No hard feelings," she answers. "Just mind your manners next time, buster, or I'll deck you!" She balls up her fist and holds it in front of his face, smirking.

Miss Val calls them back in just as they've launched into another round of rippling laughter.

Act One begins again with Fritz, the only boy in Intermediate ballet, joining Clara in front of the stool/ Christmas tree. The boy keeps pulling Deanne's hair, even though he was only supposed to do it once in the choreography.

Paige and Brindle enter and greet the Stahlbaums first—followed by their five children. After curtsying, they usher their charges toward the stool/tree and Brindle circles behind the hosts while Paige exits to change. Annie and Sophia come on next with five kids, followed by Julie who brings three more. Once everyone has come on, the "adults" socialize while the children point upward at the pretend tree, *chassé* around in a circle, and play *Duck Duck Goose*. Fritz chases Clara around the outside of the small circle, slipping on a sweater haphazardly left in his path. The little ones laugh hysterically as he trips, regains his balance, and continues to run around again. Even the "adults" are losing it.

Miss Val has to stop the music and call them back to order. She claps her hands. "Okay, class!" Then she puts up her hands to quiet them. After walking the youngsters through their parts correctly, without music, they begin the segment again.

The rehearsal proceeds with periodic interruptions for coaching. Paige knew this rehearsal would be a little chaotic, being the first time they all get together. But they are making their way through the dances, albeit slowly.

"May the battle begin!" Todd later shouts. He stands center stage with a crooked plastic sword and stabs the empty sky. "I love this part!"

Deanne laughs from her place seated on the floor, downstage right. "You're such a nut!"

"Anything for you, my dear." He bows deeply to her and the little kids laugh and squeal from their line, sitting across the front, now as the audience.

"Okay! Enough, already," Miss Val commands. "Here we go!" She laughs and turns to the stereo.

A single instrument begins to play. JP, the gymnastics assistant, prances around where the other rats will be, spooking Clara and pretending to be a dozen small rodents. The actual ones won't be joining the full cast for a couple more weeks. Deanne pantomimes her fear as if more are approaching her.

Brindle and Paige stand in the back of the studio and watch the battle transpire. A gunshot fires and they all jump.

"That part's so much louder than it needs to be."

"I know it." Paige agrees.

The Nutcracker marches on from stage right, straight legs kicking out in front of him before each footfall.

"Smaller steps, Todd! Remember, the younger soldiers are in the same line and they have to keep up!" Miss Val shouts over the music.

He nods and shortens his stride. With an about-face, he lifts his weapon and brings it downward, signaling to the absent soldiers to throw the pieces of bright yellow foam, as cheese.

"I forgot about this part," Paige says.

The Nutcracker and the Rat King posture against each other threateningly. Only, it's more funny than scary since Todd is so much taller.

"Go Rat King!" Sophia yells. "You can do it!"

Todd mocks a quick frown at the onlookers. "Take this, you dirty varmint!"

JP calls out, "Hey, remember how tall he'll be when he's got that Rat King head on! You won't be so brave then!"

It's true, the king, played by the tallest advanced gymnast, will be a lot taller when he wears that special head. Paige remembers how awesome that thing looks. The area the gymnast sees out of is actually in the neck of the mask, covered by black mesh. *Pretty cool.*

The Rat King fakes a realistic stab to his opponent and the others cheer.

"Okay. You're on, buddy!" Todd bellows sarcastically and the fight continues.

Whether it's from hunger or something else, a wave of nausea comes over Paige. She closes her eyes briefly and takes a deep breath.

"Are you okay?" Brindle asks.

"I just don't feel that great, that's all. I think I'm still hungry."

"Yeah, that could be it."

Instantly, she thinks of how awful she felt at her dad's—after she'd eaten that pizza. *Why am I thinking about that right now? This isn't anything like that.* She continues to watch the battle unfold and then she knows why.

"Hey, remember I told you about when I got sick after eating that pizza? It felt like my insides were getting attacked—like a shootout in a cowboy movie?"

"Mm hmm."

"I think this battle scene, with the *foam cheese*—" she finger quotes these words, "and hearing the gunfire, brought me back to that memory. Not pleasant, for sure."

"No. I'll bet not." Brindle looks on as the Rat King falls. "Hey, I've got an idea!"

"What's that?" Paige turns to face her.

"Let's get together and make a really delicious, healthy meal together!" Brindle's smile lights up her entire face.

Paige lets the thought register. "But when? Thanksgiving is coming up so soon, and then our performances aren't that long after that. Hmm."

Paige watches Miss Val sit down on the stool by the stereo. *She's probably worn out.*

"Well, let's see—"

"I know!" Now Paige is grinning. "Let's do Thanksgiving together!" She grabs Brindle by the arm excitedly.

"Yeah! We could make a super yummy gluten- and dairy-free vegan meal for my family and yours!"

The two of them jump up and down like a couple of little kids.

"Hey," Miss Val calls. "Keep it down over there, will you?"

Paige talks more quietly now. "It's just my mom and me this year. My sister's not coming home for Thanksgiving because they only have two days off and finals are coming up soon."

"She goes to Berkeley, right?"

"Yeah. So, let's ask your mom after class, okay?"

"You got it, sista," Brindle says, giggling.

Finally, something culinary to look forward to. I don't know much about this new way of cooking, but maybe Brindle does and she can show me.

Paige tosses a simple green salad: lettuce, tomato, cucumber, green onions, and sprouts. *It needs something else, but what?* She searches the fridge, yet again, but nothing pops out. Mom walks in through the kitchen door with a bag of groceries.

"Hi, Mom. Did you get anything good that might go with salad?"

"Um, maybe." She begins pulling items out of the sack and sets them on the counter. A small can of stuffed grape leaves plunks down next to the salad bowl. "How about this?"

Paige studies the picture on the can and smiles. "Yup, I believe this will do just fine." She opens it and lays the petite green rolls in a star-shaped pattern on a small blue plate.

"Very pretty," Mom says and finishes putting away the groceries.

The two of them sit at the little round table to enjoy a quiet midweek dinner.

"We're still going to that women's march in January, aren't we?"

"I think so. Do you still want to?" Mom looks up from her plate.

"Of course. My history teacher brought up the *Me Too* thing and I've been thinking about it ever since."

"I'm glad she's talking to the class about these things. Did you know only about 9 percent of sexually abused teenagers ask for help and it's usually not from a teacher or other adult?"

"That's pretty scary. But, you know, not everyone has a psychologist for a mom."

Mom laughs. "Well, there is that."

Paige wonders if she should ask this, or not, but decides to anyway. "Do you think Dad is sexist?"

Mom stops chewing. "Well—why do you ask, Paige?"

"I don't know. Maybe because he didn't really listen when I tried to tell him about how I eat differently now. He just—" She sets her fork down and tears at the napkin in her lap. "It's sort of like, *he* knows best, or something." She places her hands on each side of her plate. "Is it because he's a man and I'm a girl? Or is it because he's my father?"

Mom leans forward and puts a hand on top of Paige's. "He's probably a little sexist, but not nearly as bad as a lot of men. I think he was raised in a way that encouraged him to simply put himself first, regardless of gender."

Paige ponders this idea as they finish their meal. *I guess we can sometimes look back and see where our actions are actually coming from. Maybe Dad did grow up that way, as an only child. Deanne's an only child, come to think of it. And she seems extra concerned with pleasing her father. At least, that's what she told us last year.*

Deanne had broken down, right outside the studio, just after a rehearsal for *Giselle*. It started to make sense why she wanted the lead role so much. *But it's still confusing. We're all so complicated.*

13

NIGHTMARES

Brindle

Prepare for takeoff by pushing off the floor with your entire foot, finishing with the toes. Ride the leap through the air—navigate smoothly while lifting the torso and chin. Plan the descent and land through the foot, ending with the heel. Decelerate gracefully.

"Please, Dad. Can't you just take me home for an hour? I'll do the dishes." Brindle continues to plead with her parents to take her home to the canyon. She misses it so much it hurts. Last time they went, she'd sifted through the ashes where her upstairs room had crashed through the dining room, looking for anything that could be salvaged. *Almost nothing.*

"We just went day-before-yesterday, Brindle. We're tryin' here," Dad answers. "Maybe tomorrow. I think that volunteer Buddhist group is coming with a tractor to help clean up the area."

Mom comes into the kitchen, pulling on her sweater. "Hey, did the big walk-in dumpster get delivered?"

"I think so," Dad says. "That's where the tractor will come in handy."

"There sure is a lot of debris. I can't imagine how long this is going to take." Mom coughs and folds her arms tightly across her chest. "Brrr. It's starting to feel more like fall, isn't it?"

Taz parks himself at the table and opens a box of cereal. Willow cuts a bagel in half and pops it in the toaster.

"Fifteen minutes, guys. You don't want to be late for school." Mom closes the box of cereal and returns it to the cupboard.

Dad grabs two containers from the refrigerator and stuffs them into his satchel. He kisses each of them on the cheek and leaves in a hurry so he won't be late to deliver his morning lecture at the college.

After dropping off Willow and Taz at school, Brindle and Mom head down to San Diego to pick up land and building documents from County Records. Proving what they had before the fire is becoming a never-ending task. While Mom performs the title search, Brindle will be occupied at the big downtown library. She'd said it was for a paper she'd been assigned through her online homeschooling, but it's also to research ways they might be able to move back home sooner. She's selected Henry David Thoreau as her topic of study, and once there, scours the shelves for insightful material. She finds a biography and a book by Emerson, who wrote about Thoreau. But her real focus is going to be an actual book by Thoreau, *Walden*. She has a couple hours and decides to dive right in. There's a nice, comfy chair by a window and she nestles down into it.

As she reads about his quiet life at Walden Pond, she immediately feels an affinity with him. Her *Walden* is the canyon she knows as "home." He writes about his solitary walks in the woods and it makes her ache for those trails through the creek bed. Sometimes he would spend the evenings listening to the fish jump in the pond and the night birds that hearken to her own appreciation of the owls, poorwills, and bobcats that used to serenade her nights.

An hour-and-a-half passes before she looks up and stretches her legs. *Ouch, a little stiff.* Standing up, she twists left and right and then wanders to the restroom, more for the sake of movement than anything else. After checking out the *Thoreau* books, she returns to the chair, pulls *Little Women* from her backpack, and begins rereading the novel.

The village of Concord, where the story takes place, is fairly close to Walden Pond, so she's beginning to get acclimated to the general area, albeit vicariously. *Maybe someday I'll go visit.* Jo and her sisters spent a lot of time, it seems to Brindle, enjoying the beautiful natural surroundings as well as playing make believe and reading. *Why aren't more families interested in being out in nature? Why does everyone want to spend their hours shopping and going on Instagram when there's such a rich life available right outside?*

She lays the book on her lap and leans back, staring out the tall, narrow window. Traffic busily flows below, like merging rivers. An old purple bus, decorated with butterflies and peace signs, stops at the traffic light. Some of the windows are painted over. When the signal changes, and the colorful work of art moves away, dark lettering across the back catches her eye. She squints to make out the words.

HOME SWEET HOME

How fun is that? It might be interesting for a while, to tour from place to place, but I'd probably miss home too much.

And then, it hits her. She dumps *Little Women* into her backpack and pulls out one of the books about Henry David Thoreau. Maniacally flipping pages, she stops at a drawing of his little cabin in the woods.

It's a tiny house! If he could live that way for a whole year—in the snow—then our family can certainly survive in this Southern California climate!

She reads about how he harvested his own lumber for building and gets excited by his musings about living simply and sustainably. *He was ahead of his time!* Then reality sinks in.

We don't know how to build and my parents don't have time. They both have to work for a living. And how would we be able to build a tiny cabin and then a regular house? That may not get us back to the canyon any sooner, after all.

She snaps the book closed with an air of defeat. *It was fun while it lasted.* She hadn't felt that excited in a while, and now, that was gone again.

When she gets a text from Mom, she gathers her things and meets her out front. Next on their list is a stop at Target for socks and underwear. They all need more since the fire and these aren't exactly the kinds of things that have been donated.

The two of them walk in the store and are greeted by Christmas carols and holiday decorations.

"It's not even Thanksgiving yet," Brindle says in disgust.

"Socks and underwear. Anything else?" Mom looks determined.

"Nope. Let's make a beeline for them, okay?"

Mom, unfortunately, thinks of a few other things they need, which lengthens their stay. *Finally*, they emerge outside into the elongated shadows cast across the parking lot.

"Mission accomplished!" Mom says, a little too triumphantly, and they hustle to the Subaru. "We just need to stop for gas. Hmm, maybe we should get takeout for dinner, too. Chinese?"

"Sure," Brindle says. "And then can we *please* go home?"

"You know we're on the same page, Brindle. I don't like having to spend the whole day in the city, either. But the others will be hungry, too, when we get back."

When they're *finally* on their way home, and headed up the mountain road, Brindle's head begins to pulse. By the time they arrive, she's got a full-blown migraine.

Ugh, not again. I should've taken something. Every time I go to the city, I get a headache. Too many people, too many cars, and everything covered in cement or asphalt. There's no fresh air.

She passes Dad as he comes out to help Mom carry in the purchases and heads into the kitchen for aspirin. The plastic container clatters to the floor after it slips through her fingers. *Luckily it wasn't open yet.* She picks it up and wrestles off the lid, while her head continues to pound. Mom and Dad come in and set the bags on the table as Brindle swallows the small white caplets and forces some water down her throat.

"I'm going to bed." She hears Mom tell Dad about her headache, but it's beyond her to stop, listen, and then respond. *I just have to check out. Now!*

A flat, barren landscape stretches before her. Everything is in shades of gray, no color. The ground begins to shift, then moves in wavelike formations—pushing up a row of sand, carrying it forward, and then releasing it into the next ripple. It goes on and on and on. A deep, monotone sound drones on without stopping. The effect is nauseating and unnerving.

Brindle sits up abruptly, out of breath, and a line of sweat runs down her back. She shivers and shakes her head, trying to orient herself.

What the—?

Flipping on the lamp beside the bed, she looks around the small bedroom. Next to her, Willow faces away in peaceful slumber with more than half of the covers pulled around her.

That girl always has all the blankets. And she never has any trouble sleeping. So unfair.

She reaches up and rubs her temples. The headache is still there, around the edges, but much diminished. *What's going on?* This is not the first time Brindle has dreamed about this moonscape. *I want it to stop. I'm so sick of this.*

She begins to cry—softly whimpering. Tears stream down her lightly freckled cheeks, and she leans her forehead into a balled-up fist, willing the headache to go away. Then the burnt landscape comes back into focus: blackened skeletons of former trees, mounds of twisted metal and warped corrugated roofing, broken hunks of concrete missing from their former home's foundation....

Why did it have to happen to us? My favorite place in the world is ruined and now we might not even go back? Why?

Brindle wipes her eyes with her T-shirt and hangs her legs over the side of the bed, searching for her slippers. Finding them, she wiggles her toes into the hand-me-down Uggs, throws an oversized jacket around her shoulders, and shuffles out of the room. The dog dish slides across the floor when she accidentally kicks it and she grabs the kitchen counter for balance.

"Bloody rat's nest in a rainstorm!"

Taz stirs on the couch and she quickly goes outside. Nutkins comes over and nudges her with his wet nose, wagging his tail excitedly.

"You're the best, buddy." She squats down and hugs him around the neck. "What do you say we go out to the swing, eh boy?"

She kisses his muzzle and stands up, before zipping her coat and continuing out to the backyard. The swing seems to welcome her and feels almost like a friend. Moving slightly forward and back makes the nearly full moon change shape through the branches of the huge eucalyptus tree. She closes her eyes and takes a deep, rewarding breath, her natural wonder returning.

Thoreau must have spent many a night reclining in the woods, contemplating things that really matter. She adjusts her position and leans into the side-chain. Nutkins perks his ears as a siren moves through the distance. *Somehow… Some way… We've just got to move back home and get our lives back. My life is certainly not meant to be here.*

"What do think, Nutkins? You wanna go home, too, don't you?"

The dog's eyes shine up at her, reflecting the moonlight, and his tail thumps the ground.

"I knew it. You do want to."

She pushes off the ground with her feet and slowly starts pumping. The moon flashes, strobe-like through the leaves, as she swings higher and higher. Thanksgiving pops into her head and visions of turkey and mashed potatoes come into focus. But these are quickly replaced with images of tofu and hearty vegetables.

I wonder if Paige will like the stuff we make together for Thanksgiving, whatever it's going to be. I better start looking at recipes pretty soon.

"Okay, Nutkins. I gotta go back to bed. Thanks for being such a good friend." She returns to the house, relieved that her mind feels a little more settled now, and thankful she has Thanksgiving, at least, to look forward to.

14

THANKSGIVING

Paige

You are what you eat, so make healthy choices!

Someone's knocking on the front door. Paige is still in her Mallard duck pajamas when she waddles through the living room. *What time is it, anyway?* The clock on the mantle chimes nine times, answering her question as she gets to the door. *How could I have overslept?*

"Good morning, Brindle." She yawns. "I'm so sorry I'm still in my pajamas. My alarm didn't go off."

"No worries, it's fine." Brindle comes in smiling, followed by Mr. Val. "We brought supplies for our feast. Should we put them on the counter?"

Paige nods and points, yawning again. "Yeah, I'll go change real quick and be right back."

"Good idea, Paige," Mom says, coming in through the kitchen door from the garage.

"What were you doing out there?" Paige asks.

"Just cleaning out the car. Would you care for some coffee, Jethro?"

"No thanks, I've got to get back to help Val with our fire insurance paperwork. It never ends."

"I'm so sorry you have to deal with all that—and in the middle of *Nutcracker* season! I'm sure it's overwhelming." She pulls a mug out of the cabinet and shuffles over to the percolating coffeemaker.

"Well, it is what it is, I'm afraid," he says, scratching his head absentmindedly. "What time shall we arrive for the vegan Thanksgiving feast?"

Paige glances at Brindle. "Two o'clock, right?"

Brindle nods and begins pulling vegetables out of the bags as he leaves, arranging them on the table. "Bye, Dad."

"I'll be right back," Paige says again, meaning it for real this time. She heads down the dark hallway to her room. Finding a clean green T-shirt, she pulls it over her head and puts on a pair of old jeans—ripped at the knees.

After brushing her teeth and wrestling her unruly curls into a ponytail, she feels more ready to begin the adventure of helping Brindle make a very nontraditional Thanksgiving meal. The dishes will contain no gluten, no dairy, and no meat. A challenge? Yes! Impossible? No! *We're going to create a masterpiece.*

"*Voilà!*" Brindle sings with a flourish of hands, presenting a colorful array of fresh vegetables artfully displayed on the table. "Aren't they beautiful?"

"I'll leave you two to it," Mom says and leaves the room.

"Wow. They really are." Paige moves around the unusual patchwork and studies the unfamiliar shapes. "What's this?" she asks, pointing at some dark green leaves with lighter-colored, bulbous ends.

"That's kohlrabi. It's related to cabbage and Brussels sprouts and can be cooked or eaten raw. It's supposed to help gut health and all sorts of good things," Brindle answers.

"Oh." Paige can't help but crinkle her nose a little, even though there's not much smell. "What about that?" She gestures toward something that resembles a brain, semi-wrapped in leaves.

"Purple cauliflower, which, by the way, is packed with antioxidants!" Brindle follows Paige around the table with a smile growing on her face.

How does she know all this stuff? "Don't get too excited now, Brindle." Paige chuckles at her new friend.

"Oh, wait until you see the recipes I marked in these cookbooks!" Brindle laughs.

Paige steps back and studies the younger girl, by two years, who now seems older than her. *I think Brindle is the most interesting nerd I've ever met.* "Well, all right then. Let us begin!"

Brindle shows her some of the recipes she'd found. Paige gazes at the delicious-looking items displayed in the photos. *Garlic and nutritional yeast oven roasted cauliflower* lies colorfully in the baking dish, to which they, apparently, are going to add kohlrabi. *Stir-fried vegetables and tofu with rice noodles* looks so good Paige can almost smell it. And, the *gluten-free pear pie* is to die for, according to Brindle.

These sorts of foods have never looked or sounded all that appetizing before. But now, her stomach is growling.

Oh yeah, I didn't have breakfast yet.

Paige opens a cupboard and pulls out a bag of raw cashews, her new standby, to munch on in hopes of curbing her hunger pains so they can focus on cooking.

"We've got a lot of prep work to do first," Brindle says. "Do you have a colander and a few large bowls?"

Paige drifts from cabinet to cabinet and pulls out anything that might prove useful. "Okay, how many are we feeding again?"

Brindle furrows her dark bushy eyebrows and concentrates. "Seven? Just you and your mom and the five of us, right?"

"Yup. So, how many different dishes are we making?"

"Well, let's see," Brindle begins. "That depends on which ones we decide on."

The next two hours pass in a blur for the two chefs: rinsing, chopping, and combining. One side of the sink is piled high with dirty pans and bowls, and bits of greenery litter the surfaces and floor. Brindle gingerly steps around the debris and puts a tray in the oven.

"Hopefully, the cauliflower and the pie can bake together. They only require a five-degree difference in temperature, so I think we'll be all right."

Paige sets the timer on the stove and they begin to prepare the ingredients for the stir-fry. By one thirty, things are looking pretty good.

"We better clean up, Brindle! Your family will be here in half-an-hour!"

"Oh, my gosh!" Brindle laughs.

Mom comes into the kitchen wearing a pretty dark-brown skirt, white blouse, and flowered vest.

"You look nice, Ms. Smith."

"Thank you, Brindle. It looks like you girls need a little help to be ready in time. Would you like me to set the table?"

"Yes, please!" Paige answers. "We'll clean up this stuff and get the dishes in the dishwasher. Okay, Brindle?"

"Roger that." Brindle giggles. "Sorry, I don't know where *that* came from." She laughs again.

"I'll be right back," Mom says and leaves them to it.

Paige brushes the veggie remnants off the table into a large plastic bowl and a Brussels sprout rolls over Brindle's foot. She runs over and kicks the sprout, sending it flying over the table into the fish tank by the window.

"Oh, my gosh, Paige. Those poor guppies!" Brindle shouts, covering her mouth with her hands.

"You should see your face right now, Brindle! You could be an actress." Paige goes over to the aquarium and rescues the floating sprout from the hungry fish. One of them nibbles her fingers as she pulls the morsel out of the water. "Ouch!"

Brindle laughs again and ducks as the wet green ball flies past her head into the sink, and they both crack up uncontrollably.

"Score!" Paige skips over to retrieve the traveling Brussels sprout and deposit it into the metal compost container on the counter.

"It sounds like you girls are having far too much fun cleaning up," Mom says, reappearing in the kitchen.

"We are, Mom."

"Don't worry, Ms. Smith. We'll start cleaning up for real now," Brindle says, grinning and grabbing the sponge by the sink. "We'll have this place ready in no time."

An hour later, they sit down to dinner. The kitchen is fairly clean, the table is set, and all are comfortable in the dining room, passing around the unique Thanksgiving dishes.

"This looks absolutely fabulous. You girls really did yourselves proud."

"You'd better taste it first, Dad," Brindle says, passing the platter of stir-fried vegetables with tofu.

"Well, I'm sure it's all quite delicious," Miss Val says. "I'm famished and can't wait to try it all."

Paige looks around at all the happy faces sitting around their unusually crowded dining room. With just Mom and her, there's a lot of eating on the fly. "This is nice. I'd like to offer a toast."

Everyone picks up their mug of hot apple cider and looks at Paige.

All of a sudden she feels self-conscious, but pushes through and gains a little more confidence when she looks over at Brindle. "To new friendships and good food."

"Here, here," Mom says, and the others repeat it.

The only sounds for a bit are clinks, scraping of utensils on plates, and slurping from Taz as he drinks his cider.

"What's that?" Willow asks, pointing at the colorful display on the tray in the center of the table.

"You've seen that before, remember? We had it two weeks ago." Brindle stares at her sister.

"Cauliflower?"

"Uh huh. With kohlrabi and nutritional yeast. What do you think?"

Willow glances over at Miss Val, who gives her a stern look. "It's better than I thought it would be."

Taz accidentally drops his fork on the floor, creating a sharp clatter. "Oops." After retrieving his utensil and grabbing another, he adds, "I kind of like it. It's different—but it's pretty good."

"Way to go, son," Mr. Val says, patting the young boy on the back. "Good for you."

"It's delicious," Miss Val affirms. "Great job, girls."

"Yes!" the grownups agree.

Wow, we actually pulled it off. I could never have done this alone. Thank goodness for Brindle; she's amazing. Paige raises her mug to her and they clink cups and continue with one of the best meals she can ever remember.

When dinner is finished, they each enjoy a piece of the warm, freshly made pear pie topped with a dollop of almond ice cream. The whole feast has far surpassed anything Paige could have possibly imagined for a completely vegan Thanksgiving.

"I think this is the first full meal I've eaten—in months. I'm stuffed."

"Me, too," Miss Val says.

The adults volunteer for cleanup duty while Willow and Taz head outside. Paige offers to show Brindle the piano in the living room since she's heard that she plays.

"It looks so new. Is it okay if I try it?"

"Of course." Paige gestures toward the sleek piano and settles onto the couch.

She watches Brindle slowly sit down and get situated on the bench, collecting sheet music and stacking the pages neatly beside her. As if in silent meditation, she stretches her fingers and pauses.

Brindle has the most beautiful, slender hands.

When the first notes drift from the piano, Paige startles. *Where was I?*

The melody and harmony blend gracefully, leaving Paige breathless. She's never heard the piece before, yet some of the phrases are familiar—like hiking on a trail you know, but are not sure where it goes. After Brindle plays the last note, it lingers and Paige smiles, not wanting it to end. Luckily, her friend does not release the foot pedal, which enables the sound to continue until it slowly fades away.

Paige closes her eyes and takes a mental video of the last few minutes before breaking the silence. "How did you learn to play like that?" She puts a hand over her heart. "It was so beautiful."

Brindle turns to face her. "I don't know." She shifts on the bench. "I've been taking lessons for a long time. Well—not since the fire, though."

"How do you practice now?"

"I don't. We don't have a piano anymore. Hopefully someday."

Brindle looks so sad. So vulnerable. "I hope soon. You're too good *not* to be playing."

"Well, thanks." Brindle drops her chin and runs her fingers along the smooth wood of the sleek-lined instrument. "I do miss it." She smiles and stares at Paige. "I'm just glad I got to play this one today. It's nice."

"Hey, are you okay? I mean," Paige pauses. "Really? That music you just played—"

Brindle stares straight ahead, as if the words haven't reached her.

Paige walks over and places her hands on Brindle's shoulders. "I'm here for you if you need to talk."

"I know," she finally responds and pats one of Paige's hands. Brindle sets her fingers back onto the keyboard and begins to quietly play again—as if the melody is her voice.

Paige doesn't move.

"Life's just really hard right now, you know? I really miss our home." The notes continue. "And for you, too, isn't it?"

Paige struggles to follow Brindle's train of thought and then gets it. "Oh, yeah. You mean with my dad?"

"Mm hmm. And him not respecting your food issues?"

"Yeah. But I really do miss him, though."

Brindle stops playing and stands up. "I'm sorry. We're quite a pair, aren't we?"

Paige's mom comes into the room, leading the group. "How about a concert?"

Paige gives Brindle an apologetic look and watches her mentally shift gears.

"Okay." She begins to play a lively tune from the musical, *Annie*, and before long, they're all singing together.

"Tomorrow! Tomorrow! I love ya tomorrow! You're always a day away."

Taz enthusiastically dances around the living room, since he doesn't know the lyrics. When the song is finished, they all applaud.

"I'm so glad that thing is finally getting some use. I don't think it's been played since my ex-husband left. Thank you, Brindle, for bringing it back to life."

Brindle smiles, but still looks a little sad. It's getting late and Miss Val thanks them for hosting a wonderful Thanksgiving.

"And I'd like to thank our two chefs for their marvelous culinary creations. Everything was so tasty." Mr. Val pats his belly appreciatively.

"It *was* pretty yummy. I learned a lot today *plus* I had a great time!" Paige walks over and gives her new, good friend a hug and walks them to the door.

"Me, too." Brindle helps her family carry some of the leftovers to the car.

As they drive away, Paige realizes how tired she is. *Being a chef must be an exhausting job.* But she notices she's feeling pretty good. No unhappy digestive issues. *Maybe I should eat like this all the time. But it's so much work and it takes so long. This has been the best Thanksgiving ever.*

15

Tying Up Loose Ends

Brindle

*Be prepared—so you can enjoy
the performance week!*

Brindle readjusts the mask with her wrist, carefully trying to avoid touching it with her ash-covered glove. Once the square-framed wire sieve is full, she lifts it up and begins to shake out the fine contents into the growing pile on her right. Suddenly, a tarnished metal lump becomes visible on the screen and she carefully picks it out of the other gray material.

What in the world? She twirls it, awkwardly, between her fingers and brushes off the debris clinging to it. *It's heavy for its size. Oh—my little piano!* She holds it up toward the sunlight. "You're actually still kind of beautiful. A bit tarnished, but now just a different kind of pretty."

"Whatcha got there, Brindle?" Dad asks, looking over from the opposite corner of their former house.

"The piano Christmas tree ornament you and Mom gave me for Christmas that year, before I saw the real one in the living room." That had been an amazing Christmas, first unwrapping the tiny package, thinking *that* was her present, and then walking downstairs and being surprised by the antique upright grand standing in the living room. *In all its beautiful glory!* Her eyes tear up with the memory.

"That's great, honey. I hope you find more treasures."

She tucks the miniature piano into her coat pocket and slowly runs her fingers through the ashes, searching for other nuggets—or maybe it's just the meditative movement that somehow soothes her. *I miss my piano so much I can hardly stand it. We'll probably never be able to get another one like that.* She sits back on her heels and thinks about playing Paige's piano on Thanksgiving, but it wasn't the same. It was more modern and had a rather ordinary sound. *Nothing like my old upright grand.*

An hour passes as the two of them sift through various sections of the ghostly remains of their home.

"Hey, Dad? When can we move back here? Hasn't it been long enough?"

He stands and leans back, stretching, pushing his hands against his lower back. "I don't know." He straightens and kicks at the ashes around his boots. "There's still so much we have to figure out." He pauses again. "It may not make sense to rebuild here.

We may want to go somewhere else, like maybe closer to Aunt Mary's or something." He looks over to her. "We'll see."

What? "But Dad!" Brindle bellows. "We have to move back here! This is our home!" Fear rips through her and she chokes back more tears. *He can't be serious, can he?*

"We don't even have a house here anymore, Brindle. There's a lot to weigh."

Brindle rises, tearing off her mask and throwing her gloves into the mess, and runs up the road into the burnt creek bed. Charred branches scratch her face, but she pushes through anyway. Out of breath, shutting her eyes tightly every few strides to squeeze out the tears that block the blurry path ahead and stumbling over burned roots, she makes her way to her favorite boulder. It's her sanctuary. She careens toward it, reaching her arms forward, and falls against its cold surface.

She turns her back and leans her full weight into it, to catch her breath, and sobs uncontrollably. "Why, why, why, why, why?" The sky, with pinkish cumulus clouds, doesn't offer an answer. And neither does the rock. A covey of quail scuttle by under the unburned bushes surrounding her. *How come these didn't get scorched?* This buckwheat still has its brown and crème dried flowers. Listening to the quail muttering around her, she can't help but smile. *There is still life here.* And for that, she's grateful.

She parts the branches, ducks through to the far side of the boulder, and climbs up the steep incline, to the natural seat halfway up. *Home sweet home. There's no place like home.* She closes her eyes and loses track of time. Eventually, Dad finds her—he usually does—and they walk down the dirt path together.

That evening, Taz begs Brindle to read *Polar Express.*

"Again? I just read it to you last night *and* the night before that." She knows he prefers her to read to him, instead of Mom or Dad, for a couple reasons. They don't really have time these days, plus she usually loves making the characters' voices distinct and dramatic.

"Pleeease?"

He's so irresistible with those big blue puppy-dog eyes and cute little pout. "Okay, but just once tonight. Not twice like last night, all right?"

"Yes!" he yips and bounds over to jump onto his sofa bed.

Brindle slides next to him, opens the book to the first page, and begins to read.

"On Christmas Eve, many years ago, I lay quietly in my bed. I did not rustle the sheets. I breathed slowly and silently. I was listening for a sound—a sound a friend had told me I'd never hear—the ringing bells of Santa's sleigh."

Taz interrupts here, as usual. "But he did hear them, huh?" he asks.

"Yes, he did," Brindle answers and smiles at her cute little brother. *If only my life could be this simple.*

Sunlight streams in through the studio windows, adding cheer to the rehearsal space.

"*Estoy tan feliz de que nuestro concierto casi está aquí! Y tú?*"

Brindle pauses to decipher Sophia's Spanish. *I am happy that our concert is almost here.* "Sí, yo también! Did I do it right?"

"*Sí, muy bién.*"

The three musketeers laugh.

"Would you like to try now, Deanne?" Sophia asks.

"No, I'm good. But thaaanks," she exaggerates. "And yes, I'm super excited, too, that this is our last full rehearsal."

The Advanced gymnasts, who play the soldiers, are goofing around with their plastic swords while JP passes out bright yellow foam wedges.

"Yummy yummy," one of the rats says, pretending to gnaw on the fake cheese.

Deanne rolls her eyes. "So childish."

"Oh, cut 'em some slack, will ya?" Annie jokes.

"Okay everyone!" Mom calls. "May the Rat Battle begin!"

As the solo instrument begins to play, the young rats prance around the stage with their hands out in front and wrists curved, not quite even with the other. Some of them accidentally bump into each other, but carry on with their *ratty* scurrying. The soldiers stand at attention in a line across the back.

With the first volume change, one of the rats plants her feet in a wide second position, raising both forearms—creating a right angle at the elbow. This quick movement is performed downstage left, in front of Clara as she makes her entrance. She feigns fear and covers her mouth. Then the rat continues on, prancing strangely. When the next change happens, another rat does the same, spooking her a second time.

Clara turns around and around dizzily, circling her arms above her, and the rats copy behind. The soldiers march forward into a line in the center when Clara and the rats are finished with their twirling. At last, each group faces the other and prepares for battle. The Rat King and Nutcracker posture and dance against each other humorously.

Brindle laughs despite seeing it all before, because each time it's a little different.

The Rat King performs his *sauté, step hops* around in a circle and then Todd does the same in the opposite direction. His jumps look a little lopsided and Jack yells, "Clean it up, dude!"

Everyone laughs.

"That's enough from the peanut gallery!" Mom calls over the music, and the battle continues.

Todd menacingly draws up his sword and aims it toward Jack, who's over by the front desk next to Randi. He lowers it sharply, signaling to his young soldiers to throw their fake cheese at the rats. Upon doing so, the little rats run forward and grab the chunks before scurrying back to their own line of defense. More posturing and sword fighting ensue as the two main characters threaten to kill each other.

When the two groups run forward and pick up the rope for the tug-of-war segment, Deanne announces from her place on the floor, "This is my favorite part!"

They all laugh when the rats fall down and frantically kick their legs in the air, as the noble Nutcracker and his team win the round. The two leaders circle around each other and when Deanne, as Clara, throws her slipper at the Rat King, she misses and accidentally nails Todd in the head.

He wails sarcastically and stops temporarily. "Why you—"

"You're lucky it was just a fuzzy slipper and not a *pointe* shoe!" Deanne teases.

Mom claps loudly to get their attention. "Carry on, don't stop! We don't have time to repeat this one today!"

The Rat King drops to the ground after Todd pretends to stab him; the little ones droop their heads and bodies in sorrow and then drag their beloved leader off stage right. The Nutcracker sends his soldiers away when their task is completed, and they salute and march off in the opposite direction.

Before proceeding forward, he dusts his hands and lifts his nose in the air. In a British accent he says, "Good riddance to those vermin and now, my lady, may I assist you to your feet?" He doesn't have the Nutcracker head on for this run-through, but he operates with a ridiculous-looking stiff neck, mimicking the head.

The cast cracks up and Deanne buries her head in her hands. "Oh brother," she says when he approaches.

Mom pauses the music and gets everyone back on track. Brindle looks on as Deanne and Todd regain their composure and walk in a circle together to begin their duet.

The group proceeds through the various dances that provide entertainment for the Nutcracker prince and Clara while they sit on their imaginary throne. For now, they are perched on the low balance beam in front of the other gymnastics equipment stored behind the curtain, which is now pulled aside. They skip some of the dances because those groups won't be practicing with them until dress rehearsal.

Brindle walks over to begin the *Waltz of the Flowers,* thinking about how Mom has this down to a system. *If they only knew how much time she saves everyone by only including the necessary groups.*

She and Paige wait out the intro in the music and then dance on from stage left, moving across the diagonal. Midway through the piece, during the *piqué turn* circle, Paige bumps into her from behind and accidentally trips her. Almost falling, she scrambles to catch her balance and finishes the last *double tour* with a *single* instead.

"I'm so sorry!" Paige pants as they move forward into a line.

"It's fine. I'm okay." Brindle continues to the right.

During the rest of the piece, Brindle senses Paige watching her more than usual. It's a little unsettling and she wonders why. *She knows the dance well enough, I think. She doesn't* need *to copy me.*

At last, the rehearsal ends and Mom sits everyone down in various places around the floor, so she can keep track of the younger groups more easily. Randi and Todd find a place by themselves and sit next to each other, leaning against the side wall. The parents file in for the meeting while Deanne and Paige pass out flyers with all the information concerning the dress rehearsal, school assembly, concert, and out-of-town performance.

The shades are pulled up in the big windows and Brindle sees the costume lady making her way with a load of colorful party dresses. She hurries outside to help her.

"Well, thank you, Brindle. I could use some extra hands." She tilts her head toward the car.

Brindle gathers an armful. "I'm happy to help."

There are Russian soldier outfits, rat attire, period party costumes, white tulle snowflakes, and beautiful dresses adorned with cloth flowers for the waltz. Brindle is intoxicated with the beauty and elegance Ms. Flanners creates. "You're so talented. These are so beautiful."

"They certainly are," Mom echoes as they come in the door with their second load. She walks over to separate two Beginning ballet students who've been messing around far too much.

The meeting gets underway, with a few parents sitting on the low balance beam, some standing, and others sitting on the floor.

"I'll try to be as brief as possible," Mom begins. "It's so exciting, isn't it everybody?" She smiles genuinely at all the dancers looking back at her. "Our dress rehearsal is Thursday evening, day after tomorrow! Can you believe it's almost here?"

Mom is doing her usual pep talk. Randi, of course, is sitting with Todd, leaning against him. And Paige is looking at me again. Why?

Mom continues dispersing information. Most of it is on the flyers, but not everyone reads them, so she has this meeting to try and cover all the bases. When Ms. Flanners starts passing out the costumes, nestled in their plastic bags, Brindle and Paige get up to help her.

"These are to stay in your parents' closet, not yours," Mom explains. "They are not to be worn until dress rehearsal. Got it?" She gazes at all the younger students authoritatively and then smiles. "These are rental costumes and must be returned in good shape after our performances, okay?" She nods, encouraging everyone to do the same. A few adults smile their approval at her tactics.

One of the little goofing off Beginners stands up and sets the dress on her head, but the plastic bag it's in is slippery, causing it to fall to the floor.

"No, no, my dear. I don't think so." Mom grabs the crumpled heap and takes it over to the girl's mother. "For safekeeping," she says, shooting the girl a semi-stern look.

After the meeting, Sophia comes over to Brindle. "Hey, I re-read your dragon story. It's really good. I liked it a lot." She shifts her two costumes over to the other arm. "What gave you the idea? It's so creative."

Brindle shrugs. "I don't know. I just couldn't sleep, I guess." *Maybe it was the fire, but I don't feel like going into that right now. I'm rather sick of talking about it. Everyone is always asking.*

"I liked it, too. Will it continue or is it finished?" Deanne asks.

Brindle shrugs again. "I don't know. I don't have time right now since all our performance stuff is this week."

Sophia wiggles excitedly. "Can you believe our dress rehearsal is so soon?"

"I know!" Deanne says and then joins her mother outside.

When Sophia leaves, Paige comes over. "I couldn't help but overhear. You wrote a story?"

"Yeah, a while back." Brindle drops her water bottle into her ballet bag. "It's not a big deal or anything."

"Could I read it?" Paige looks at her intently.

"Maybe," Brindle hesitates. *I usually only share my stories with Deanne and Sophia, no one else.* "Really, it's not all that great. I just couldn't sleep one night so I got up and wrote. Kind of like journaling?" *Will that hold her off?*

"I'm sure it's really good, Brindle. You're so smart." Paige points to the Saxon Algebra book sticking out of her bag. "It's probably much better than you realize."

Brindle bends over to pick up her things. "I don't know. Let me think about it."

Paige smiles at her. "All right."

Brindle straightens up, holding her belongings.

"It's okay, I understand if you're not ready to share it. And—I want to thank you again for making that fabulous Thanksgiving feast with me. I've been feeling so much better these days and you're part of the reason. I guess I just needed to learn about other things I could eat. I think I'm finally eating enough—of the right things."

"I'm glad. It was delicious, wasn't it?"

The girls walk outside giggling and reminiscing about their successful culinary adventure together.

16

Here We Go

Paige

Figure out the details—it's dress rehearsal!

The afternoon is unseasonably warm and students are milling around the quad with no jackets, only light sweaters. Paige has been looking forward to lunch all morning for two reasons. One—Randi will be joining her, since Todd is playing basketball. And two—she's packed delicious leftover macaroni and cheese, with gluten-free noodles and soy cheese. When her chemistry teacher lets them out five minutes early, she hurries to her locker and then secures their favorite lunch spot, on the tree well beneath the magnolia.

"Hi Paige," Randi says as she dumps her coat and backpack on the seat and sits down next to her. "Math was a bear today. It's so confusing. I don't know how I'll ever pass the final." She unzips her bag and pulls out a PB&J.

"You know, I *could* help you. *If* you could ever spare time away from Todd." Paige pulls the lid off her container and digs in.

"Really? Oh, thank you. Thank you! I could really use it."

"Well—when would work for you?"

The popular group of stuck-up girls flings open the door to the dance room and catcalls to the football players hovering nearby. By the time Randi finally answers, Paige is halfway finished with her lunch.

"How about next Monday after school, once our *Nutcracker* performances are over?" Randi has finally unwrapped her sandwich.

Paige takes another bite, watching the girls playing stupid and flirting with the boys. "Okay," she says. "How can they think they're so cool, anyway? And those guys are *not* the brightest. I just don't get it."

"But most of them are pretty cute, don't you think?" Randi takes her first bite.

Paige stops chewing for a moment and then answers honestly. "I don't think they are." She's not really sure why, but she's never found teenage boys to be that attractive.

"Hey, remember that pact we made with each other last year? The one about trying not to badmouth anyone, especially if they're not around to defend themselves?" Randi is staring at her.

Paige laughs. "Yes. It was my idea, remember?"

"Mm hmm. Of course I do." Randi takes a sip of water and clears her throat. "Hey, I'm sorry I haven't been hanging out with you as much as I used to. I guess having a boyfriend sort of does that, huh?" A nervous giggle escapes.

"I know. And I do understand. But—I miss you."

Randi puts her arm around Paige and pats her opposite shoulder.

It feels so good. It was always great being around Randi. No wonder I miss her so much.

"Hey, do you think anybody here at school cares that Todd and I are together? I mean, you know, that he's black?"

Paige looks around at the students milling around their small-town high school and answers, "Yeah, probably." She thinks back to when she overheard that group of girls talking about them, but doesn't feel like bringing it up. "But I wouldn't give it a second thought. It's *their* problem if they have an issue with it."

"Yeah, I agree. Once in a while we do get some weird looks. But for the most part, everyone seems fine about it."

"That's good," Paige says. "We probably need more displays of open mindedness, whether it's interracial couples, same-sex relationships, or even those that just want to be left alone, for that matter." Again, her focus is drawn to the popular kids who only seem to care about their appearances and what *looks* cool.

Miss Val hurries around the stage—fixing this, moving that, and delegating tasks.

She looks a little frazzled. I hope everything is all right.

"Jethro! Would you go get that other red rope out of the truck? I forgot to bring it in."

He climbs down the ladder and descends the stage stairs while the light guy pushes the metal brakes up off the wheels of the scaffolding before pulling it to center stage. The technician's assistant climbs up with a large, bulky light and proceeds to hang it from the bar above, using a wrench to tighten it securely.

Paige looks up at the hodgepodge of various-sized lanterns decorating the stage sky. "Looking good!"

The guy waves from above, and smiles. "We aim to please."

"That's what I like to hear," Miss Val says, squinting up at the light. "Could we aim that one down here? This looks like a dark spot."

"Will do," the technician responds, and then instructs his helper how to accomplish that.

Paige lugs her stuff into the girls' dressing room, on stage left, and haphazardly hangs her costumes on the closet rod.

"How long have you been here?" Randi huffs and puffs into the room as if she's been running. "I thought we were going to be late! Todd and I had to run an errand after school." She proceeds to drop her pile onto a chair and then starts digging through her ballet bag.

"I just got here. I had to take a makeup test in precalculus." Paige pulls off her pants and begins rolling on her ballet pink tights. "So, are you excited, Miss Sugar Plum Fairy?"

Randi giggles. "Of course I am! But I'm kind of nervous, too." She takes off her shirt and throws it on top of her heap and then puts on a nude-colored leotard. "Be right back," she says and disappears into the bathroom.

Arriving together, the three musketeers crowd in and claim their own sections of the dressing room.

"Hey, Sophia. Try to stay organized, okay?" Brindle says. "We all have to share the space, you know."

"You're such a neatnik," Sophia teases, while kicking her things into a tighter pile.

Thank you, Sophia," Paige says. "Hey, are you guys ready for this?" She slips on her dress for Act One.

"I am!" Deanne says. "And I suppose you're twitterpated. Am I right, Paige?"

They all laugh.

"Of course, how'd you guess?"

"It wasn't that hard. You made such a big deal about that word last year. Where did it come from again? *Bambi* or something?"

"I guess, but I learned it from *Winnie the Pooh*. And it was owl who said it."

"My sister says it's from *Bambi*, too," Brindle says.

"Yeah, she's probably right," Paige says.

"I loved *Winnie the Pooh*. And, you know what?" Brindle asks, rhetorically. "It was loosely based on the writer's son, Christopher Robin. At least, I think that's how it went. I don't know, it's been a while since I read about it."

"Well, whatever," Deanne says. "Hurry up and get ready so we can warm up."

Miss Val starts the rehearsal twenty minutes late, due to a technical delay with the sound. "Okay, everybody. Places!"

The parent volunteers usher their groups to where they're supposed to be and the party scene unfolds. In the March Dance, Brindle's hand rests on top of Paige's, and they walk forward in the double-line procession. When they turn to face each other, they smile, moving toward the back and curtsying and then toward the front and curtsying again. Stepping on the beats, they each hold one arm upward and gallantly walk around the other clockwise. Then they repeat counterclockwise.

Paige looks around the stage. It's all so formal and sophisticated. At the end, they all finish in a V-shape, opening toward the back, kneeling and leaning away from center. They have to hold this position a little longer than is comfortable, since the gap before the next music is longer than Miss Val had hoped for. But it still works. It gives them time to catch their breath before saying goodnight to the Stahlbaums and head home with their sleepy children, along the streets of London.

The rehearsal has been going on for almost an hour by the time Act Two begins, since a few things had to get repeated. After all, that's what dress rehearsals are for— to iron out all the kinks before the big performance. Deanne and Todd, as Clara and the Nutcracker prince, sit on the throne in back center, after the battle scene and their first duet. The enchanted couple is dazzled by the snowflakes, candy canes, Spanish Dancers, Arabian Dancers....

Randi's boyfriend had wanted to play Mother Ginger, but couldn't since he'd already be on stage as the Nutcracker. Instead, the curtains open onto an Intermediate dancer's dad fanning his painted pink cheeks and admiring his brown curls and bonnet in a hand-held mirror. This part is traditionally played by a man, even though it's a mother-type figure.

Paige stares and snickers. *He's hysterical.*

He lifts his gigantic skirt and all the little squirrels run out from underneath into lines on each side of him. As they tumble forward, he continues to fan himself and invite laughter from everyone on and off stage. The little Preschool gymnasts have to keep being shown where to go, and Miss Val and JP are there to guide them from behind the side wings. This piece has to be repeated so there will be half-a-chance it'll go smoothly tomorrow.

What a crack up....

When the Chinese music comes on, the curtains open and a huge dragon dances in place while the Intermediate gymnasts perform acrobatics. The under-rigging of the gigantic, colorful costume is made up of five parent volunteers who weren't afraid to be onstage. At least as long as they would be covered up, Miss Val had said.

Brindle leans over and whispers, "This is way better than that traditional dance they usually do in *The Nutcracker*, isn't it?"

Paige smiles at her and agrees. "Without a doubt. And it looks like your little brother is getting better at cartwheels, too."

Just then, Taz runs over to their side of the stage and shoots Brindle a gigantic smile.

She laughs. "Yeah, and he absolutely *loves* that dragon."

"Close the curtains," Miss Val tells the stage manager standing next to her.

The woman is a former student who helps out at all the Dance Centre's performances. She presses a button on the device strapped to her belt and speaks softly into the headset. "We're closing the curtains, so stop the music now." She nods to Miss Val, but she's already gone to help steer the dragon people offstage.

Randi and Jack make their grand entrance, as the Sugar Plum Fairy and the Cavalier. The pair of them, in their royal white costumes festooned with hundreds of sparkling sequins, command attention as they perform the *pas de deux*. She smiles and twirls and he grins and supports.

Paige can't help but chuckle at the image it portrays. *Randi's dancing really well and I'm glad to be supportive—even if she hasn't needed me much these days. Hmph. Pull it together. She's still a good friend.*

After a wobble coming out of a triple *pirouette*, Randi *développés* her right leg in *a la seconde* magnificently high. After this, it's Jack's turn to shine. He launches into his *jeté entournants* circle and goes higher with each jump.

They look like they're having fun. I hope they can pull it off this well tomorrow.

As usual, they run through the *finale* a couple times since this is the first chance everyone can practice it together. It's nine o'clock by the time they call it a night and Paige is exhausted and hungry.

What do we have at home that I can eat fast and then go right to bed? Nothing comes to mind as she gathers her things from the dressing room and says goodnight to her ballet family.

Mom's there in the auditorium when Paige comes out and she's relieved she doesn't have to call and wait for her to get there. She goes over and leans her head on her shoulder.

"You look tired, my dear." Mom pats her head gently.

"I am."

"Bye, Paige," Randi says, walking out with Todd, hand-in-hand. "See you tomorrow morning."

Paige manages a smile and a wave as she and Mom make their way to the doors. She takes one last look up to the stage where Miss Val's entire family is bustling around, getting it ready for the assembly tomorrow morning. A few volunteers are also pitching in and Paige feels confident that tomorrow will be a good day.

17

THIS IS IT!

Brindle

Embrace the dancer within!

The dress rehearsal had gone as well as could be expected. There's always a bigger cast for this show, so a lot more details had to be worked out. As soon as Brindle finishes brushing her teeth, Taz is at the bathroom door, clutching none other than *The Polar Express.*

"Please, Brindle? Just once tonight?"

"Ugh. No, Taz. Not tonight. I'm sorry, but I'm exhausted."

He pouts, and Bonnie and Clyde race by him when they hear Mom opening the bag of cat food in the kitchen.

She shakes her head and Dad comes to the rescue, dodging the feline balls of fur. "It's really late, son, and you all have your assembly performance in the morning. It's off to bed, I'm afraid." He escorts his little first grader to the living room couch and pulls the covers down for him.

It's so hard to say no *to him.* Brindle goes into the bedroom, where Willow is already asleep. She slips under the sheets, turns off her lamp, and sincerely hopes that she, too, can fall into a dreamless sleep and be well rested for the big day tomorrow. *Two performances in one day! Here's to hope.*

Brindle carefully hangs her costumes on the closet rod and lays out her ballet pink tights; nude, spaghetti-strapped leotard for underneath; *pointe* shoes; accessories; and makeup. She finds it much easier to think and function at her best if things are neat, clean, and organized.

The door to the dressing room swings open and Annie enters, bringing with her the fumes of a hair salon.

"Phew!" Brindle practically chokes. She waves her hand in front of her face. "What did you do, use a whole can of hairspray?"

"Well, hello to you, too, Brindle." Annie teases. "Miss Val said not to spray it backstage, so I put it on at home, before I left." She sets her fashionable beige tote on the counter and drapes her costumes over it. "I'm sorry." She smiles. "It is a bit strong. I won't get this kind next time. Another model raved about it, so I thought I'd give it a try."

The door opens again, bringing in fresh air to diffuse the scent. "How is your modeling going? I haven't heard you talk much about it lately. Hi Sophia. Hi Deanne."

"It's good. I'm doing a shoot next weekend for a commercial."

"Really? How awesome is that?" Sophia chimes in. "What's it for? Do you know?"

"No, not yet."

"It must be so glamorous being a model. I can certainly see why they like you. You're so chic and exotic looking," Sophia continues.

"Is it because of your heritage?" Deanne asks, finding a spot to call her own.

"You mean, being half Chinese? I don't know," Annie answers.

Mom pokes her head in the door. "Have you seen Willow?"

"I just saw her coming out of the bathroom," Julie says, squeezing past. "Oh, and Miss Val? Paige is in the bathroom in the auditorium and she doesn't sound good."

"What do you mean—doesn't sound good?" Mom waits.

"I think she's throwing up."

"Uh oh." Mom leaves in a hurry.

"Oh, poor Paige," Sophia says. "I hope she's okay."

Deanne starts pulling on her tights. "Well, if she's throwing up then she's probably *not* okay."

∾❧∽

When warmups are over, Paige emerges from the dressing room and shuffles over to the Advanced group of main characters.

Randi approaches. "Are you feeling any better?"

Paige puts her hand to her lips to cover a burp. "Not really."

Deanne stares at Paige's feet. "Aren't you going to wear your *pointe* shoes?"

Paige looks down and shakes her head. "No, I don't think so. It's too much work to put them on, and even more to dance in them."

Mom walks by. "Good choice, Paige."

"Do you think you caught a virus or something?"

"No, not likely," Paige says, turning around to face Brindle. "I was so hungry when we got home last night that I grabbed a few of my mom's chocolate chip cookies she had stashed in the cupboard. If I haven't learned my lesson by now, there's probably no hope for me at all."

Mom stares at Paige. "You probably don't feel much like doing the ballerina doll part then, do you, with those quick changes off stage in the middle of Act One?"

Paige shakes her head.

"Brindle, do you know the ballerina doll dance? You've seen it enough times, over the years, haven't you? It's less than a minute long."

Brindle's jaw drops. "I think so," she says slowly.

"Can you do it then?"

"Probably?" *All of a sudden my heart is racing.* "But will the costume fit?"

"Close enough," Mom says. "Problem solved. At least this is the school assembly, not our evening concert."

True enough. She's right. Annie agrees to get the costume and lays it out, off stage right, where Brindle will now be changing at warp speed, just after she comes out with the kids into the party scene.

Too bad it's not a villainous role. Those parts are so much more fun.

Randi gently pats Paige's messy bun. "Don't be so hard on yourself. This is *so* not like you. I want the happy-go-lucky Paige back."

"Me, too." Paige smiles weakly. "Hey, I'm starting to feel better already."

Before Brindle has a chance to really wrap her head around what's just happened, the festive ballet begins in all its colorful splendor. She finds herself shaking a little when she enters from stage left. She curtsies to Mrs. Stahlbaum, extends her hand to Dr. Stahlbaum, then ushers her children over to the tree and quickly ducks behind it to go make her first costume change.

Luckily, JP's there to unzip her dress and hand her the ballerina doll bodice with the affixed tutu. She wiggles it over her hips, not difficult because it's a little big, and then pushes her arms into the puffed sleeves.

"Wait, Brindle!" JP whispers. "You gotta wear this." She presses the tiara onto Brindle's head and squeezes her shoulders, smiling. "All set? Go get 'em, girl!"

Herr Drosselmeyer makes his humorous entrance and then slowly drags the frame, covered with bright Christmas wrapping, out onto the stage. Brindle and the two other dolls creep behind the contraption trying not to be seen. Drosselmeyer is the toymaker who brings three life-sized dolls to the party in the Dance Centre's version. One is a ballerina doll, now danced by Brindle. Another is a clown doll, who is a Contemporary student. And the last is a Russian soldier doll, one of the Advanced gymnasts. This year, a friend of Jack's agreed to play Drosselmeyer. *Mike is a good addition to our cast.*

Brindle can only see a little bit of Mike's posturing before it's her turn. She counts the music in her head and senses him coming near. She turns away and bends over at the waist. Then, his hands are on her hips and he's pulling her toward center stage, but she can't see where she's going. *A boy is pulling me by my hips and facing my rear end! Ugh. But I better not think about that right now.*

He turns her to face front, still bent forward at the hips; she knows, from watching Paige do this, that he's winding the imaginary key on her back. Her arms are raised, at right angles at the elbows, and she jerks upward in three separate movements. *This is fun! I can't help smiling, but then I remember I'm supposed to have a stone face, like a doll, so I freeze the half-grin and try not to forget again.*

Next are four *pas de basques*. And then a stiff *sauté, tombé, glissade, pas de chat*. Brindle continues to hold her arms fixed. She remembers the short traveling pattern to the left, the échappés, but forgets one of the connecting steps and has to improvise. *Good thing it's a solo, no one to compare to.* Then she *bourrées* backward and her arms come up to high fifth—almost. At last, she collapses forward at the hips again, spent of her wind. Drosselmeyer pulls her back and sends her off stage.

That was fun!

Brindle barely makes it back in time for the March Dance, so at least the music is able to keep rolling.

Later, after the toy maker gives Clara the Nutcracker doll gift, her jealous little brother, Fritz, grabs it away from her, spins around, and pretends to throw it down on the floor. In reality, it's a gentle drop, so the figure is not actually harmed. Of course, poor Clara is heartbroken, but Drosselmeyer comes to the rescue and performs his strange magic to fix the Nutcracker.

The colorful costumes, festive music, and beautiful dancing entertain the young students in the audience and they clap loudly at the end of Act One. During the Rat Battle, as everyone calls it, Brindle notices Paige lingering in the dressing room.

"You don't want to watch it, do you?"

"No, not today."

The others go out to watch from the wings and Brindle decides to stay behind with Paige.

"It's probably safer in here anyway, away from wayward swords and flying cheese, right?" Brindle jokes. "Hey, do you still want to read that story I wrote, about the dragon?"

Paige's face brightens into a smile. "Yes, of course I do."

"I'll email it to you later."

The dressing room door quietly inches open. "The coast is clear," Randi laughs. "You can come out now."

Toward the end of Act Two, after the *Waltz of the Flowers,* Brindle watches Randi and Jack nail the shoulder sit. She beams up there, like it's the best place in the world to be. *They're certainly more confident than they were last spring. I wonder if I'll ever get to do a stunt like that. Or dance anything other than a supporting role. Oh yeah, I did just get to do a little solo!* Brindle shrugs it off and runs out to join everyone in the *finale.*

When the curtains close for the last time, Todd yells, "Yabba-Dabba-Doo!"

"That's not very prince-like," Randi scolds jokingly.

Jack, as the Cavalier, puts his arm around Randi, as the Sugar Plum Fairy, and says, "And that's why *we* are royalty and *he* is not." Then he proceeds to stick his nose in the air and Randi follows suit.

Everybody cracks up and continues bantering as they disperse to change out of their costumes and return to school.

"Call time is five o'clock this evening, everyone. Don't be late!" Miss Val announces. "Hey, Paige, will you be able to go home and take a nap?"

"Yeah. My mom's picking me up. And I already feel a lot better."

"That's good. Drink a lot of water, okay? Maybe that'll help flush out those cookies—if that's what it was."

Paige follows Brindle into the dressing room. "Hey, thanks for doing the ballerina doll dance. I don't know how I could've done it. I was moving pretty slow."

"My pleasure. It was really fun!" Brindle smiles at the feeling of dancing the fun solo.

"Hopefully, by tonight, I'll be up to doing it. We'll see, okay?"

Brindle nods and the girls finish changing and arrange their things for the evening. What a busy day, and it's not even half over. Her family will tidy up here and reset the stage, then go out for a late lunch.

It's an all-day affair for us. But I don't want it to end—this is a blast!

18

NUTCRACKER CONCERT

Paige

Smile, you're on camera!

Paige takes extra pains in laying out her ballerina doll costume *just so*. She doesn't want to leave anything to chance, especially after the way she felt this morning. Her stomach is not in as much turmoil as it had been, so she now looks forward to performing all her parts—perhaps not at 100 percent, but with as much gusto and pizzazz as she can muster.

"I'm glad you're well enough for your solo, Paige," Brindle says. "But in all honesty, I have to admit it was really great for me to get to do it and I'll miss performing it again. Good luck, though!" She laughs.

Deanne waves her over to the dressing room. "Do you still want help with your hair?"

Brindle leaves and Paige picks up the pretty pink costume by its puffy white sleeves. Images of Brindle in this outfit dance like snowflakes and gently settle around her. *Brindle is so graceful—much more so than I'll ever be. Why didn't she get the part?*

Paige hugs the outfit to her chest, sensing its former warmth, and concentrates on being able to fulfill the role as well as her new friend. *Why do I feel so weird?*

Paige is knocked out of her reverie when JP offers her a chair for the tutu.

"Oh, thanks." Paige joins Randi at the rosin box.

"I can't seem to get enough of this stuff." Randi wipes one foot at a time, breaking the small crystals that will help her shoes to not be as slippery on the stage floor.

"Neither can I."

They turn to listen as Brindle, Deanne, and Sophia belt out their traditional good luck chant.

"Pat a cake, pat a cake, dance if you can!
Yes ma'am, yes ma'am, of course we can!
Graceful, flowing, nailing every step!
We can, we can, dance with pep!"

Randi and Paige laugh at their comrades' antics, but then clap their appreciation.

"The three musketeers got it right, don'tcha think? Time to shine!" Annie says, walking by and giving each of them a high-five.

On the other side of the front curtains, patrons of the ballet, mostly parents and family members, mingle sociably in the auditorium until the light technician flickers the house lights to signal everyone to their seats. Mr. Val is running sound, so Paige knows it's him slowly fading the background music. The entire cast is where they need to be for the beginning. The narrator parts the front curtains, with the stage manager's help, and goes out onto the apron to address the packed audience. The same man has been doing it for as long as Paige can remember. He was a student's dad a long time ago and, evidently, loves doing it so much that he keeps coming back. *Plus he's good at it, and funny.*

Just before the curtains open, JP loudly whispers, "Remember the Dancespiration: Smile, you're on camera!"

During the party scene, Paige notices a large present under the tree wrapped in kitty cat paper. *That's got to be Randi's contribution.* She tries not to laugh.

At the end of the act, Paige, Brindle, Sophia, Annie, and Julie line up off stage left. When the mid-curtains close, they each begin their trek across the stage, staggered, bringing their sleepy children along with them—making their way back home on Christmas Eve. Annie leads with her charges and they yawn, as they're supposed to, and meander off the other side. Brindle comes out holding hands with two of her small children and the others lag behind. One of them, her little brother Taz, lies down in the center as if to go to sleep. The audience laughs and Brindle pretends not to notice. Then Drosselmeyer comes along, sees the sleeping boy, and looks around for his parents. Not seeing anyone, he hoists Taz over his shoulder and the procession continues moving until the last have traversed the lonely streets of London. They are now, supposedly, nestled all snug in their beds, while visions of sugar plums dance in their heads—according to

"Twas The Night Before Christmas," anyway. Paige smiles. She always thinks about that during this part.

The narrator goes out again so the crew can set up for the battle scene—lay out the tumbling mats and tape them down, move the tree and props off stage, and open the back curtains all the way to expose the giant Christmas tree painted on the backdrop. While this is going on behind the curtains, the young performers from Act One exchange places in the audience with those in Act Two.

After Paige changes into her flower costume, she watches the Rat Battle from stage left. She chuckles, grateful she can now enjoy the scene. After all, it *is* quite entertaining.

Brindle comes over to join her behind the left side wing to watch Todd and Deanne dance their *pas de deux*. Clara *bourrées* forward while her prince walks, as regally as he can, opening his arms toward her. He grasps her hips from behind and lifts her higher with each step: *sauté, tombé, glissade, soudechat*. Deanne sails through the air as light as a feather.

"She's beautiful," Brindle says, staring.

"Yeah, she's so—ballerina-like!"

The two girls giggle and Miss Val shoots them a stern look.

Paige whispers, "Anyway, it must be nice to have such a ballerina body. I've always been big-boned, and more intellectual than physical."

Brindle turns to her. "Nothing wrong with that."

Paige keeps her focus on the dancers. "No, I suppose not. It's just the way it is."

Later, the curtains open to Mother Ginger preening herself. When the little squirrels run out from underneath his/her voluminous skirt, the crowd goes wild. The little preschoolers run higgledy-piggledy all over the mats before finding their correct places for tumbling. Once they start rolling and chasing the giant inflated acorn, the audience can hardly contain itself while the chaos continues.

"They steal the show every time, don't they?" Paige says.

"They sure do," agrees Brindle.

Their *Waltz of the Flowers* goes better than it ever has. In spite of how awful she felt earlier, Paige now exudes happiness and well-being. In the end, the Sugar Plum Fairy and the Cavalier wave goodbye to Clara and the Nutcracker Prince.

All of a sudden, it hits her. *Our big performance, which we've worked hard on for so long, is over! It's bittersweet. On the one hand, our nervous worry is gone, but so is our hopeful anticipation.* The last performance is tomorrow afternoon, up in Jasper, but that's kind of low-key. This *is our big hurrah.*

As usual, they go out in groups for the *finale*, with the main characters coming on last. The audience is very enthusiastic tonight. During their rounds of bowing, the crowd cheers and applauds like it will never end. But eventually it does and Miss Val sends the groups off with their parent volunteers while the Advanced dancers head to the dressing rooms to change and get ready to greet their awaiting fans in the auditorium for the reception held in their honor. Juice and cookies for all!

"You ready?" Randi hovers over Paige who's sitting at the makeup counter.

"Oh, are you waiting for me, kind madam?" Paige puts her hand over her heart.

"Indeed, I am. *And,* I'm glad you seem to be back to your normal, chipper self tonight."

"We did great, didn't we?" Paige beams up at her best friend, wearing a huge smile.

"Uh huh. Now, let's go find you some gluten-free cookies, shall we?" Randi sets her ballet bag on the floor, away from the door. "Come on, let's go. Just leave your stuff here."

The two girls walk across the stage as Mr. Val, JP, and one of the techs are lowering the backdrop.

"Nice job, girls," JP calls.

They thank her, in unison, and proceed down the steps and out the stage door into the auditorium. Immediately, the video guy stops them to get their thoughts, on camera, about how the concert went.

Randi smiles, nervously. "Good, I think it went pretty well. Don't you, Paige?"

"Good?" Paige counters. "It was absolutely fantastic! And super amazing! And now I'm sad it's over."

"Well," the man says. "You still have one more show tomorrow. Isn't that right?"

Paige ponders her previous thought and decides to upgrade it. "Yes, in fact, we most certainly do. And we're going to be fabulous there, too."

The two of them wander into the crowd as he moves on to his next target.

"Someone's in a good mood." Randi laughs and then gets sidelined by her parents.

Paige starts to follow, but someone taps her on the back.

"Dad! I didn't know you were coming!"

He leans in to hug her and the room spins. *First— no contact for months, then—dismissing her food issues as irrelevant, and now—this?* She closes her eyes and gives in to the moment.

"I wouldn't have missed this for the world. Of course I'm here!" He pulls back and grasps her shoulders.

She doesn't know what to say, so she just stands there with her mouth agape. *He missed my last performance, so I'm not sure what, "wouldn't miss it for the world" really means here.*

"Well? Aren't you glad to see me, Paige?"

Why is he making this all about him? This is my *performance.* "Yeah, of course I am." She nods her head on automatic.

"I think you danced very well tonight." He spins her under his arm and starts leading her toward the doors. "Let's you and I go out somewhere. What do you say?"

Paige applies the brakes and turns to face him. "This," she presents the crowded auditorium. "This is our cast party and I'm part of it."

He stands back, astonished. "But, I'm going back home right after this."

His pleading eyes haunt her, but she remains firm. "I'm sorry, Dad, but we're all celebrating now, after all the hard work we've put in. I appreciate you coming to see me. I really do. You can stay here and celebrate with me. I'd like that."

Here comes his winning smile *again.*

"Well—I really better go. I'll call you. "

"Hello, George. I didn't realize you were coming this evening." Mom has suddenly appeared.

"Of course I'm here. Our youngest seems to have danced her way into all these people's hearts. However, mine was first," he insists. "Well, I guess I'll be off now. Good night, dear. You did dance beautifully." He nods to them both and exits the building, looking back once with a pained expression.

Mom wraps Paige in the biggest bear hug ever and rocks her back and forth. "You were fabulous, Paige!" She smiles warmly. "Just try to let bygones be bygones, whatever that means for you, and enjoy your special night. And, oh, I almost forgot. These are for you." She hands her daughter a bouquet of red and white roses.

"Thank you, Mom. They're beautiful!" Paige sticks her nose into the plastic wrapping and inhales. "They smell good, too."

"Well, they're nowhere near as beautiful as the way you danced tonight. You totally shined! Now, run over and celebrate with your ballet family, okay?"

Paige perks up and *chassés* over to join Randi and Annie.

"On to the gluten-free cookies!" Paige declares.

"Yummy cardboard," Todd teases, presenting his back to Randi.

She hops on board, pointing toward the tables in back. "Onward, my faithful steed, to the gluten-free and gluten-heavy delicacies beyond!"

Paige and Annie follow along behind.

"One more show, eh?" Annie asks.

And Paige answers, "Yup, one more show."

Paige tries her best to get back into the spirit of the evening, but the whole *Dad* thing continues to nag at her. Everyone's in good spirits. *And we should be. This was a great show and I really do love my ballet family. They're the best. Every last one of them.*

19

WHERE DO WE GO FROM HERE?

Brindle

*Be flexible, we don't always
get the nicest stage.*

The Jasper High School gym is not the ideal venue for *The Nutcracker*, but it's the biggest place available here. Tourists flock to this cute little mountain town at all times of the year—especially for pie, music, art, and theater. In the fall, they come for apple picking and cider. There's the *Jasper Lilac Festival* and also the *Daffodil Show* in the spring. Summer offers the *Weed Show* and Fourth of July parade, while the winter brings snow for all the city dwellers who descend on this place for an old-timey winter wonderland. And snow is what they have this weekend.

On a crowded Saturday like this, Brindle is glad their group arrives in the morning, to set up and run through the ballet before the matinee. By lunchtime, the whole town is crawling with tourists.

Brindle finds a place up high on the bleachers to eat her lunch and read more from *Walden*. She turns to the bookmarked page and slowly slips into the natural world of Thoreau's words. He speaks of the downside of working on the land that one owns, becoming its slave. But, he, too, labored to build his own cabin in the woods and to catch and grow his own food. Brindle feels his connection to the land and to the natural environment and it makes her yearn that much more for her beloved canyon.

Mom and Dad, Brindle notices, have finally gotten a chance for their own lunch break and they settle on the bottom bleacher, below her. Most of the other dancers have gone out with their parents to grab a bite at the local establishments before the matinee.

"What if they won't let us rebuild?" Mom asks. "You know, the county may not interpret the building history records in our favor?" Mom takes a bite of her sandwich and chews like it's not very appetizing.

Brindle stops reading and perks up, privy to their private conversation. *What?*

Dad shifts his baggie to one hand and wraps his other arm around her. "We'll figure out something. We just have to weigh all the options."

"Jethro!" Mom yells under her breath. "So, you think we should just sit around, *weighing our options,* and let the bureaucrats downtown decide our fate for us?" She leans away from him and he withdraws his arm.

Mom's right, in a way. But Dad's approach is usually nicer to be around. And lately, I've noticed she's got a lot of fight in her.

"Well?" she asks, pointedly.

He leans forward and takes a bite, chewing in silence while she stews. "Let's just get through today," he finally says.

Get through today? But this is our life they're talking about! Our home and our happiness! All of a sudden, Brindle feels such an affinity with Mom. *We have to fight this—whatever* this *is. I need home and I think Mom does, too.*

If the topic wasn't over, it is now, because several families come in through the gymnasium doors, letting in gusts of frigid air that swirl around the cavernous space. Their children run over and join Willow and Taz on the tumbling mats.

Their lives seem so uncomplicated. They just summersault and cartwheel through their issues. If only it was that easy for me.

In Act Two, during the *Waltz of the Flowers,* Brindle forgets the strand of roses for her costume and then slips badly on the glossy gym floor when her *piqué* turns carry her off the roll-out marley floor. She falls down onto her left side and sits stunned.

Brindle holds her breath. *Am I okay?* She pushes herself up off the floor, more wrestler-like than ballerina, and walks around in a circle, ballet-style, which is not part of the choreography. Distracted by her earlier worries about their future home, whatever that is, she struggles to remember the choreography. *Focus, Brindle, focus!* Finally, she resumes her steps with the music and finishes with a bit less flourish than usual.

"What a trooper," Mom whispers from the wing.

I sure don't feel much like a trooper right now. I've felt like throwing up ever since overhearing my parents' conversation at lunch.

Jack steps forward to take Randi's hand and they begin the *pas de deux.* Their dancing is totally in sync and beautiful to watch. Clara and her prince rise from their throne, where they've had to sit patiently and appear entertained by the kingdom of sweets, to wave farewell to the royal couple. When the rest of the cast enters for the *finale,* the audience claps and hollers. After all, this is their last performance of the season and it's much more relaxed than the concert last night. It's mostly parents, grandparents, and families, but there are also people from this community who have come for the cultural occasion.

Mom comes out to take a final bow with the cast and presents the group one last time—her smile big and genuine.

By the time Brindle's family is all packed up and leaving the parking lot, snow is fluttering all around. Dusk closes in as the world is turning white.

"How's your leg, Brindle?" Dad asks. "That looked like a pretty hard fall."

She rubs her leg before answering. "I'm fine. It's only a little sore."

"Can't we get out and play in the snow?" Taz asks.

"Yeah! Please?" Willow begs.

Mom clutches the truck steering wheel and adjusts the wipers to the next higher speed. "Not tonight. It's getting harder to see and it's just about dark."

Dad adds, "*Nutcracker* costumes don't exactly make for the best snow gear, you know. Let's come back during your winter break from school."

"That's a good idea," Brindle says. *Usually, I'd be up for the snow, but somehow, I don't feel like myself. I just want to go home. But since that's not an option right now, I'd just as soon eat dinner, curl up in bed, and finish reading* Walden. *But first, I'd better read* Polar Express *to Taz. Again.*

"No! I won't accept that!"

What is going on? Brindle props her head up off her pillow. The clock reads 2:13 a.m. She can hear Mom and Dad's muffled voices through the thin wall.

"You're just tired," he says. "Let's talk about this in the morning, okay?"

"But I need to figure this out now. You know that. This whole thing has been put on hold for too long. I barely got through *The Nutcracker.*"

"I know," he groans. "If we must, we must. I'll put the coffee on."

Brindle lies as still as she possibly can. She doesn't want Willow to wake up and interfere with the conversation that is likely going to take place right now. *And I need to be a part of it!*

She carefully pulls her legs out from under the two sleeping balls of fur and puts on the oversized flannel shirt she uses as a robe. Dad startles when she appears in the kitchen, as he's turning from the refrigerator with a carton of almond milk in hand.

"Hey, did we wake you?"

"Yeah. Sort of." *Get to the point.* "I want to be part of this conversation. I need to be," she asserts.

"Well—I don't know, Brindle—"

"Maybe she should be," Mom says, appearing from the darkened room. "I think she ought to be brought into this discussion. She's old enough, and clearly, she's very attached to the fate of our home." She strides to the counter, pours herself a cup of brew, and tops it off with a dollop of nut milk before joining them at the table.

Dad looks at Brindle with loving eyes, for what seems like forever, without saying anything. Then he clears his throat. "Brindle—we know you've been spending a lot of time studying small dwellings lately."

"How did you know?" She wipes her eyes.

"It wasn't difficult. You kept leaving the computer open to those pages. Was it a secret?"

"No. I've just been trying to find a way for us to move back home sooner. Like—live in something smaller while a new house is built?"

"As you may or may not know, Brindle, there are more than a few roadblocks to returning to our former life."

"Return to our former life?" Mom argues. "*That* isn't even possible." She turns to face her daughter. "Do you remember when I dropped you off at the library downtown while I went to County Records and did our title search?"

Brindle nods.

"Well, that's when we began to find out about all the past issues with the land grants and the current problems the county is dealing with. It's not just us. It's all the fire victims in our area."

Dad clears his throat quietly in order to not disturb Taz, who's sleeping in the adjacent room. "We've been talking to an attorney, who's looking into the details for a lot of folks here."

"I'm not entirely sure he knows what he's doing," Mom interrupts. "He keeps going back and forth as to whether or not we'll be allowed to rebuild."

"What? We have to go back!" Brindle's eyes sting, threatening tears. "Don't they have to let us, at least, have what we had before?"

Dad pauses. "Evidently—not necessarily."

"But—"

Mom slaps the table with both hands. "You know what? She's right."

Did Mom just flip?

She turns to face Brindle. "We want the same things, we do." She searches for words. "The canyon—it's the only *true* home you've ever known, right? That place is everything to us." Her eyes brim with tears, too. "It's where we belong."

Those last words hang in the air, poignant with meaning. So much so that nobody can say anything for over a minute. Brindle closes her eyes tightly and all her bottled-up emotions, kept in check to get through *The Nutcracker*, flood through her. Tears run down her chin and drip onto her hands, which are clamped into fists in her lap. Now crying freely, she opens her eyes.

Dad stands abruptly. "Wait a minute. Maybe all your searching has not been in vain, after all, Brindle! What about a trailer? There's that old one that's parked near Aunt Mary's house with a *For Sale* sign on it!"

Mom looks up at him. "Huh?"

"Oh!" Brindle says, all of a sudden.

Mom catches on. "A trailer is kind of like a tiny house, isn't it? We might be able to live in one while we build. We could probably save a lot of money that way."

"Sure! Why not?" Dad beams.

Mom reaches out to hold Brindle's hand, and then Dad's. "We *have* to go back, don't we?"

"Mm hmm." Brindle nods.

Dad interjects, "Can we legally do this?"

Mom lets go of Brindle and straightens to face him. "Forget legal," she says. "We can't fight this if we don't even live there. I say, we buy a trailer and get back onto our land. Bring the horses and goats from my sister's and we all move back."

"Really?" Brindle asks. "Can we do that?" *Can I do more than hope now?*

Dad eases back in his chair, opens his mouth to say something, then thinks better of it. When he finally speaks there's a glint in his eyes. "Yes. Let's do this!" He pounds the table lightly with his fists and raises his coffee mug to Mom's.

They clink cups and Brindle bumps theirs with her knuckles. "When can we go back?"

"How about we start tomorrow, by assessing potential trailer sites and cleaning up a little?" Mom suggests.

"Do you mean today?" Dad asks. "It's already three o'clock."

They laugh together and Mom says, "Yes, I guess that means today. Let's go back to bed and then we'll all go home and figure out what we need to do. Deal?"

"Here, here," Dad says.

"Thanks. I feel so much better now. I can't wait for tomorrow! I mean today." Brindle chuckles.

Dad wonders out loud. "What should our new house be like, anyway?"

All three freeze and then, at the same time, chime, "Logs!"

"Of course," Mom says. "After all, we are *re-building*, aren't we?"

It's almost ten o'clock by the time they've packed lunches and piled into the Subaru. The truck is still loaded with *Nutcracker* stuff and can wait until later.

They're going home! It may be just for today, so they can figure out how to do this, but Brindle is beyond happy. Her worst worries have finally been dispelled and there is now at least a game plan—of sorts.

I haven't felt this energized in months! I'm not even tired, though I should be after last night. Oh, my, I think I slept solid after our talk. No nightmares! What a relief!

Brindle takes in each scene as they drive on the dirt road: the torched tree trunks, black ash covering the ground, twisted metal remains of former vehicles, shattered glass, and then their chain link gate that stands open—welcoming them. Mom parks the car in front of the flattened house site.

The dirty yellow bulldozer that a volunteer had used to clear debris is parked in the pasture. Nutkins jumps out at the first opportunity and takes off after a rabbit. Mom closes the door and leans against it. Then she gets that mischievous glint in her eye that they all know so well, and takes off toward the tractor.

"Uh oh," Dad says. "What's Mom gonna do now?"

The three kids gather together with him, watching, as Mom climbs up onto the seat and looks back at her family.

"No time like the present to remember how to drive a tractor! Let's hope my parents' driving lessons, from however many years ago, are still lodged in my brain."

Dad smiles and shakes his head while she turns the key in the ignition and the beast roars to life. Black smoke belches from the upright exhaust pipe and Mom tinkers with the levers.

"We better give her some space so she doesn't run over us while she's trying to figure out how to operate that thing."

Willow and Taz walk over to the house site with him, and Brindle decides to rake through the ashes where the playhouse used to be. *It's been years since I played in there, but it's close to where Mom's working so I can watch her.*

The skip loader jerks forward, backward, and sideways until the inexperienced driver eventually starts to get the hang of it. After a while, Mom pulls up near Brindle and the motor shudders, then quits, bringing a sharp silence.

"Dad and I were thinking that maybe we could pull a trailer in right here, next to where the old playhouse was. What do you think?"

Brindle scans the area. "I guess it is sort of flat here."

"We'll have to use the outhouse. At least it didn't burn in the fire."

Brindle laughs. "Lucky us!" Their little wooden privy, which has served them well when they're outside working, stands unharmed under a crisped oak tree. "I'm just excited we're moving back home!"

Dad comes over with cutters and PVC pipe and starts to mend the faucet. "We'll need water to hook up to."

"That's for sure," Mom says. "Well, stand back, everybody, so I can get this pad ready. At least we'll be able to say we live here. And they can't take that from us," she says, smiling defiantly.

"And this, my friends—" Dad pauses for effect. "Is how it's done."

The tractor fires up; Dad cuts the pipe; and Willow, Taz, and Brindle sift through the ashes of their childhood.

20

FINALS

Paige

*"Happy Christmas to all,
and to all a good night!"*

Paige's stomach growls as she flips the paper to the last page of her Chemistry final. *Buck up girl, you got this.* She keeps the mantra going in the back of her mind while her main focus is on the test. Science is her favorite subject and she still wants to be a scientist—someday. The next question is about Marie Curie and she's glad she had that conversation with Brindle about the award-winning woman scientist. It helped to cement some of the facts in her brain. It also gets her thinking about women's place in the world historically, the march scheduled for next month, and the whole *Me Too* movement. *Why is it that we still have to work so hard for equal treatment?*

She finishes her last equation five minutes before the bell and uses the time to go over some of her answers.

At the end of class, the students carry their test papers up to the teacher's desk, where he makes eye contact with each one and smiles. Paige appreciates this and thinks it's rude when some of the students don't smile back, or even acknowledge him. At least *he's* trying.

"Have a nice Christmas," Paige says.

"And you, as well."

Randi is outside the door waiting for her. "Took you long enough."

"What? The bell just rang."

"We got out early, as soon as we were finished with our math tests," Randi says. "And, thanks to you, I think I did okay. Are you ready to go?"

The quad fills with boisterous teenagers, set free for winter break. "Two whole weeks off! I'm so ready!" one guy shouts over the roar of animated conversations.

"Yes!" Paige answers. "Let's get out of here."

Once in the parking lot they walk carefully, making sure some overly excited driver doesn't run them over.

"I'm so glad you can finally drive me. Maybe I'll get my license this winter. I haven't had much practice, though," Paige says, buckling her seatbelt on the passenger side. "Where's Todd? Isn't he coming?"

"No. He got hired on as seasonal help at the equipment rental place." Randi laughs. "Now he can pretend he knows something about lawn mowers and chain saws."

"Hah! He'll be good at that. He's got such a big personality."

Randi smiles and slowly backs out of the parking space, only having to jam on the brakes once, when someone guns his engine behind her. "On to the Yogurt Cave and away from this madhouse."

"Yes, indeedio! I'm starving."

Randi looks both ways and pulls into the traffic. "Hey, will they have anything you can eat there?"

"I think so. I'll find something. Besides, Brindle says she's gone there recently and she's vegan."

The shopping center gleams with Christmas decorations and Randi says, "Look how cute those antlers are on that car."

"You've always been a sucker for kitsch, haven't you?" Paige teases.

"It's not kitsch, you—you—person with no taste." Randi giggles.

The Yogurt Cave is brightly lit and festive decorations abound. The front windows are draped with elegant green garland accented with shiny Christmas balls. Lively carols play in the background and compete with the three musketeers' conversation.

"Over here, Randi!" Deanne waves.

Sophia says, "Hi guys," when they join them. "They have several specials today and they all look yummy."

Paige smiles and nods to Brindle, who grins back.

"They have a cashew yogurt today, Paige," Brindle offers. "I think I'll try it."

Paige removes her coat and drapes it over the back of her chair, next to Brindle. "Okay, sounds tasty."

Julie comes in with her mom. "How long before I should pick her up?"

"I don't know, how about an hour?" Paige guesses.

"All right then, honey. You guys have a good time."
The nice mom leaves, promising to be back later.

"So—" Paige turns to Brindle. "How'd your finals
go? Oh, that's right. You're home-schooled. How's
that work, anyway?"

"I just need to finish the online tests by the end of
the week. I've already turned in all my papers."

"Do you like it?" Paige asks, as the others go to the
counter to order.

"Yeah, pretty much. I have a lot more flexibility in
what I choose to study or write about. And, believe it
or not, I do a lot more work in this program than for
any school I've ever gone to!"

"Really?" Paige studies Brindle's sincere face. "Don't
you ever get lonely, though?"

"Hah," Brindle laughs. "Hardly! I have you guys.
But, then again, I am kind of a loner at heart."

"Oh, I almost forgot—I *loved* your dragon story. Was
it inspired by the fire at all—and losing your place?"

"Maybe. I don't think I was consciously thinking of
that when I wrote it, but when I read it later, it did
sort of seem like it."

"Well, write what you know, right?"

Brindle laughs. "I guess so. Shall we go order some
cashew yogurt?"

"Of course."

When Paige and Brindle return to the table, Deanne
is teasing Randi. "What's this I hear about you and
Todd going to the drive-in movie this weekend?"

"What? Where'd you hear that?" Randi asks.

"Oohh, you guys are going to the drive-in? You lucky ducks," Sophia says.

"*Afortunado patos?*" Brindle asks.

"Pretty good," Sophia answers. "But *patos afortunados* is probably better for *lucky ducks.*"

Deanne talks over the crowd. "Todd must have let it slip. I heard it from Marie."

"Jack's girlfriend? Are they even together anymore?"

"Who knows?" Deanne says, taking a delicate bite of her double chocolate extravaganza.

"Well," Randi answers a little defensively. "I haven't exactly said yes—yet."

"So, there you have it, Deanne," Brindle says. "Let's talk about something else, shall we?"

Paige chimes in, "How about those Chargers?"

Everyone stares at her.

"Since when do you know anything about football, Paige?" Randi asks, slapping her friend's shoulder with the back of her hand.

"Since—" she pauses. "Never." She throws her head back and laughs. "I was just trying to change the subject, in jolly jest!" and everyone cracks up.

"This is so much fun, isn't it? I mean, getting together like this," Randi says.

"I agree," Paige answers. "Why can't we always be this relaxed?"

"Probably because we usually still have finals and performances looming ahead of us to worry about," Brindle offers.

"True that," Randi says. "I'm gonna go get some water."

"Hey Paige, are you feeling better these days?" Sophia asks.

Paige takes a small bite of her softening yogurt. "Yeah, I am. Thanks for asking."

"Is it true you can't eat gluten anymore?" Deanne asks. "I don't know what I'd do without my favorite fudge cookies. I make them practically every week."

"I've been seeing a naturopath who has me avoiding gluten and dairy right now," Paige begins. "At first it looked as though I had a gluten sensitivity, but now it seems like I have an intolerance to it."

"You mean like celiac disease?" Julie asks.

Paige stirs her melting dessert. "Maybe, I don't know yet."

"Don't you want to get checked out by a real doctor?" Deanne asks. "So you'd know for sure what's wrong?"

Brindle comes to the rescue. "A naturopath *is* a doctor. They're just trained to look at the whole person, not just at their disease."

"We tried that first. Mom took me to several doctors and even the ER. They never figured out anything. At least for now, I feel better and have a game plan. So that's a good thing."

Deanne's mother pokes her head in the door and signals to her daughter.

"I gotta go. Merry Christmas, everyone!"

"Merry Christmas, Deanne." Randi smiles and they all wave.

"See you at Youth Group tomorrow," Sophia calls after her. "We're having an early Christmas party at church," she tells the group.

"Ah," Randi says.

Brindle turns in her chair to face Sophia. "Hey, did you ever finish *Little Women?*"

"Yes, I finally did. It was a little slow-going because I kept thinking about the movie."

Paige interjects, "I really liked Jo, but I wanted to strangle Amy."

"I know, huh?" Brindle nods her head. "She seems like she just wants to please everyone else."

"Do you think she really believes her only value is to be a wife? Jo's far more interesting and independent— my kind of woman," Paige says, matter-of-factly, scraping the dregs from her bowl.

"Were Amy's art lessons just a way to make her more appealing to men?"

"It could be, Brindle. Who knows?"

"Hey, let's talk about the women's march, okay?" Randi offers.

"It's next month, right? We haven't even had time to talk about it at my house," Brindle says. "Between *The Nutcracker* and trying to get our place ready for a trailer and moving our animals back, it's been crazy." She smiles and adds, "But good."

"I think school will be back in session by then, won't it?" Paige asks.

Sophia checks her phone. "It—looks—like—yes, it will be."

"I think it might be good for us to do this together, don't you guys think?" *It feels nice to have my bigger ballet family around and not just Mom and me all the time. I'm so lucky to be part of this.*

"Absolutely," Randi says. "There'll be so many people there that we'll have to get dropped off somewhere else and then walk a long way."

"Better wear decent walking shoes," Sophia says.

Julie asks, "What is this march you guys are talking about?"

"Oh, I'm sorry," Paige says. "It's a march for people to demonstrate for human rights and fair treatment."

"It's important," Brindle adds. "And it's a way we can all feel like we're doing something for the greater good."

"Can I come, too? I mean, if my mom says it's okay?"

Paige answers, "Of course. That's the beauty of it. No one is excluded. Lots of men go, too. Isn't your dad going, Brindle?"

"Last I heard, he is." She stands up and starts gathering the dirty paper bowls to throw away. "Hey, I'm just curious, have you guys read the book *Polar Express?*"

"Yeah, I love that book," Sophia says. "Our whole family does."

"Well, that's *my* latest reading. Taz has me read it to him every night. Over and over and over again."

"That sounds nice," Paige says. "I sometimes wish I had a little brother."

"I have four. Do you want one of mine?" Sophia jokes.

They all turn toward the front window when the outside lights flicker on.

"It gets dark so early now," Julie says, looking out for her mother.

Randi wiggles her little jingle bell bracelet. "I love Christmas. All the decorations make me feel so cozy and warm inside." Then she smiles bigger and blurts out, "And Christmas kittens!"

They all laugh.

Paige shakes her head. "What in the world are Christmas kittens, Randi?"

"I don't know. There are Christmas reindeer so why not Christmas kittens?"

Paige pictures a sleigh pulled by kittens and bursts out laughing. "You cat fanatic."

"But really." Randi gets serious. "It always seems more special on the years we put on *The Nutcracker*, doesn't it?"

Paige thinks about this for a moment, watching all the light-string-wrapped columns outside flash with red and white candy cane stripes. "Yeah. It does somehow seem bigger and brighter when we're helping to contribute to the holiday spirit. I think it's also because we always grow so close during it all. And it's like our family is more than just the people who live in our house. It's our whole ballet family!"

"It is." Randi agrees.

"I love you guys so much. You're the best family a girl could ever ask for." Paige stands up to put on her coat.

"Group hug!" Sophia shouts. "To the most awesome family ever!"

They move together and the whole place watches.

"Merry Christmas to y'all too!" Paige announces and the patrons laugh and cheer the girls on.

As the dancers disperse, Paige gazes at all the festive reminders of the season, pictures each one of her "ballet family members" going home, and wonders what they think about when they're all alone. Her main preoccupation this year has mostly centered around her uncomfortable stomach issues and trying to *fix* herself. Grateful she isn't suffering from constant tummy aches anymore, she now has time to ponder more interesting things. And her older sister is coming home from UC Berkeley for a whole month! Paige can't wait to hang out with her and have heart-to-heart talks with someone she can truly confide in. So many thoughts, ideas, and questions swim around in her head.

Maybe my wonderful sister can help me sort out some of them. Mom is great, but sometimes I just want to talk with someone who's still a kid—kind of. Will I ever feel like a grownup?

A Tribute

In loving memory of Dale Larson: the long-time narrator for the Ramona Dance Centre's story ballets and husband of Lori, the "real-life" costume lady.

Your resonant voice will forever be heard in our hearts as we remember all of the story ballets you narrated with humor, excellent timing and engaged, spontaneous enthusiasm. You were truly one of the most present and alive people I've ever had the pleasure of knowing.

—Love, Chi

Acknowledgements

Any work of this type requires a village. That is to say, that without the help of everyone involved, this book would not have come to fruition. My dear friends who provided editing, ideas, and support include Susan Nelson, Bo Varnado, Helen Buchanan, Pamela Stricker, Chelsea Dulaney, Kent Richardson, Henry Herz, Carmen Erivez, Ana Lajeunesse, and numerous friends and ballerinas. For the business of getting this book published and marketed I'd like to thank Monkey C Media, Susan Farese, Edwin Steen and Guy Buchanan. A special appreciation goes to Nora Read Coats for providing the wonderful cover art. And to my children: Jessie, Kali, and Chance. There are also many more kind souls who have helped bring this project to completion—you know who you are. And last, but not least, to my husband, Kent, for his ongoing belief in my abilities as a writer.

About the Author

Chi Varnado lives in the backcountry of San Diego County with her husband and a menagerie of animals. She taught dance for thirty-seven years and her own studio staged a story ballet each year—similar to the one in The Dance Centre Presents The Nutcracker! This novel is Miss Chi's fourth published book, the second in the series, The Dance Centre Presents. Visit us at www.dancecentrepresents.com.

EARLY EXCERPT FROM BOOK THREE:
THE DANCE CENTRE PRESENTS COPPELIA

BLOW OUT

Jack

Dance with love in your heart.

Jack's right foot slams down onto the brake pedal as he steers sharply toward the direction he's skidding. It had all happened so fast. He braces himself against whatever impact might be coming and time slows down.

Just this morning he'd gotten out of bed thinking this was simply going to be another typical Saturday. First—a shower; second—breakfast of champions: Wheaties of course; and then getting ready for ballet class. Dad had already gone to the garage.

Look for it in 2021

OTHER BOOKS BY CHI VARNADO

The Dance Centre Presents Giselle

THE TALE OF
BROKEN TAIL
ILLUSTRATED BY
DOROTHY MUSHET
BY CHI VARNADO